HO! MUM!!

HONESTLY MUM!!

Kathryn Lamb

Piccadilly Press • London

For Charlotte, Izobel, Ben, Daniel,
Octavia and Alexandra

First published in Great Britain in 2004
by Piccadilly Press Ltd,
5 Castle Road, London NW1 8PR
www.piccadillypress.co.uk

A catalogue record for this book is available from
the British Library

ISBN: 1 85340 714 3 (trade paperback)

1 3 5 7 9 10 8 6 4 2

Printed and bound in Great Britain by Bookmarque Ltd
Design by Judith Robertson
Set in 9.5/16pt Arial

Chapter One

Welcome to My World

MY NAME'S Maddy Mitchell and I'm thirteen and a half, which makes me about a hundred years younger than the average age of the other inhabitants of our village, Little Bunbury-on-Wee, Wee being the aptly named little stream that trickles down one side of the High Street, which is pretty much the only street, with the village green on one side and a small pond on the other, with ducks! (The fact that I've put an exclamation mark after 'ducks' shows that there isn't *that* much to get excited about in Little Bunbury – but I like ducks!) This is where I live, with my mum, above the Village Stores (groceries, post office and newsagent combined), which Mum runs. (The Village Snores would be more accurate.)

DUCKS!

Mum's most outstanding quality is that she is *nice*. Very, very *nice*. She is especially popular with her elderly customers, who drop in every day for a pint of milk, a packet of custard creams and a good old gossip (with the emphasis on 'old'). They're always telling Mum (known to all of them as Mrs Mitchell, or just 'Helen') what a lovely, well-behaved girl I am. I suppose I am. But they might be worried if they knew some of the stuff that goes on inside my head. It worries *me* too! For example, I think it's quite mean of me to think of poor Aunty Ann as . . . the Human Jelly – but I can't help it! Aunty Ann is an assembly of wobbly bits – apart from her hair, which is so stiff with setting lotion that it never moves.

MUM
(NOW YOU
KNOW WHERE
I GET THE HAIR
FROM!)

← WAVY HAIR
(WHO IS IT
WAVING AT ?!)

ME – MADDY (AGED 13½ –
THE HAIR MAKES ME LOOK ABOUT 12 !!!)

Aunty Ann is married to Uncle Nigel, who is Mum's elder brother, although he doesn't share her good looks. He has a long, hooked nose and a permanently curled-back upper lip, revealing a set of very large teeth. I am never sure whether Uncle Nigel is smiling or doing an impression of a horse. I think he is probably smiling, as he is very good-natured, like

Mum. But he doesn't say much, apart from 'Yes, dear' to Aunty Ann. Uncle Nigel and Aunty Ann, who are childless, live in a small house several doors away from us and dote on their dog, who is called Foofy.

AUNTY ANN — WITH FOOFY

Foofy is also known as: 1) Foofy-Woofy, 2) Iddums-diddums dog and 3) Mummy's darling precious huggums 'n' squeezums. I don't like what has happened to Foofy. I love animals, and when I was eight I used to have wonderful romps with a tiny, beribboned Foofy, who used to leap all over me, licking my face and ears. I blame Aunty Ann for over-indulging her pet, feeding him endless titbits and doggy treats and making him fat, short of breath and short of temper. I don't have a pet of my own (Mum doesn't want one – she says that I'm enough for her! And it wouldn't be fair to keep a dog cooped up in a flat). She agreed ages ago with Uncle Nigel

← THAT HAIR AGAIN...

UNCLE NIGEL

and Aunty Ann that I could 'share' Foofy . . . So while other children had brothers and sisters or friends nearby to play with, I had a small and increasingly bad-tempered Pekinese as a playmate.

Looking back, I am amazed that I didn't seem to mind too much about this. I was quite happy being a good little choir

3

girl, enjoying the attention and praise lavished on me by the friendly customers, especially the older ones, who have watched me grow up. ('Your Maddy has the voice of an angel, Mrs Mitchell – you must be so proud of her!' 'Oh, I am!') I was happy with the daily routine of being ferried to and from the primary school in the next, slightly larger village, Long Bunbury, by Uncle Nigel, who has an office there where he works flexible hours as an accountant. (Long Bunbury is still too far away for me to be able to see friends who live there very often.)

I can't remember the first time I thought: My life is *incredibly* boring. It may have been when I was about eleven or twelve. I think it was a feeling that crept up on me gradually, starting with a slight lessening of enthusiasm for things such as getting up in the morning, and ending with a full-blown snarling, teeth-gritting reaction at the very mention of choir practice or Monopoly. (I try not to show this too much, as I don't *want* to hurt Mum's feelings. I don't *want* to be a moody so-and-so, but I can't seem to help it . . .)

I was saved from going completely mad halfway through last term by the arrival in our village of a person of my own age! Her name is Rio de Havilland and she joined my school, St Swithin's Comprehensive, in the nearby big town of Leatherbridge. (School motto: Learning in all weathers!) We have been good friends for nearly four months (we're into the second half of the summer term),

← COOL HAIR!

RIO

and we travel to and from school together every day on ye ancient rattling school bus. Rio's cool – she's fun, friendly and popular, and she has cool hair – and I'd like to hang out with her and the Cool Crowd more when we're at school. So why don't I? The reasons are: a) We're in different classes, so I don't always see that much of her, and b) My other slightly less cool friends get upset and jealous if I don't hang out with *them* – and I don't like upsetting people (I guess I'm like Mum!).

A good reason for wanting to spend time with Rio when we're back home, apart from the fact that I like her, is that she has an older brother called Syd. Syd is two years older than me and really good at art, and I reeeeeally fancy him! (Sadly, I tend to go bright red and lose the power of speech if he so much as looks at me.) Rio and her family live in Marsh Cottage at Bunbury Bottom, just outside the village itself – I usually cycle there. Rio's parents run a healing centre several miles away, right out in the countryside, where stressed city people go to escape the pressures of modern life. I think Rio's parents are cool (but Rio says that they are

← MESSED-UP HAIR (SEXEEE!!!)

SYD

4 ME
4 EVER! (I WISH...)

only slightly less sad than most parents). They allow her to wear make-up and have cool hair and express her opinions (loudly). Rio has strong opinions (such as 'Homework should be banned!'). I find it hard to have a strong opinion. I can usually see both sides to an argument, and just when I've finished arguing for one side I start to see points for the other side. I'm a human ping-pong ball! (Not literally . . .)

Maybe I should mention the person who is *not* in my life — my dad. He left and went to Australia when I was only two, and he hasn't bothered to keep in touch. I don't know what his problem is, considering how nice Mum is, and I think she's pretty – but I don't want to get into all that right now. I expect he got married again to a kangaroo and I probably have a whole herd of half-brothers and half-sisters hopping around, all called Joey . . . *Don't worry!* I tend to have these mad thoughts when I'm getting upset – it's my way of cheering myself up. To be honest, I don't even remember my dad and I don't think about him that much.

Right now I'm more concerned about finding an excuse for getting out of choir practice tomorrow evening . . .

Chapter Two

That Friday Feeling . . .

IT IS A warm evening in early June and I am walking home from St Mary's Church after another thrilling choir practice. (No – Mum *didn't* believe me when I told her that my voice had just broken and I could no longer hit the high notes . . .)

Old Mr Battlefield hobbles past with his walking stick, smiles and raises his hat to me. 'Lovely evening,' he says. (I try to imagine how it would be if boys of my own age, or a bit older, were to start raising their bobble hats to girls – they would all end up with bad hat hair, and the girls would laugh at them. Oops! There I go – getting distracted by weird thoughts again . . .)

'Hello, Mr Battlefield.'

'Nice to see you, Maddy. Just finished choir practice?'

'Yes.'

'Jolly good. Doris and I love

MR BATTLEFIELD

7

to hear you sing, you know. We'll be there on Sunday, in our usual pew.'

'Oh . . . good!'

'Well, I mustn't stand here chatting – I must get back to Doris. She worries, you know.' Raising his hat again, he shuffles away.

Mr Battlefield and I pass each other like this *every* Friday, and every Friday we have *exactly* the same conversation. Does Mr Battlefield ever get bored or irritated? Apparently not . . . maybe some people like consistency. I feel bad for getting annoyed so easily . . .

Back home

Boc! Boc!

'Hello, darling!'

'Hi, Mum.'

Uncle Nigel and Aunty Ann are already there – they come to supper every Friday.

'Good choir practice?' asks Mum. She doesn't wait for an answer. 'Supper's on the table. Come and sit down before the salad gets cold! Ha ha!' (This is a joke. It is Mum's

I HAVE A SUDDEN URGE TO RUN VERY FAST IN CIRCLES MAKING NOISES LIKE A CHICKEN . . .

joke. She makes the same joke every time we have salad. I

have a sudden urge to go completely mad and run very fast in circles making noises like a chicken. I don't remember suffering from these urges when I was younger. I think I was pretty normal then. These days I find it hard to sit still at the supper table.)

'Stop fidgeting, dear! Aren't you hungry? I thought you liked ham.'

'Sorry, Mum – I'm just feeling a bit full.'

'Too many sweets, I expect,' comments Aunty Ann. (*She's* a fine one to talk!!! I've never seen anyone work their way through as many strawberry creams as she did last Friday whilst watching a particularly traumatic and harrowing

episode of her favourite soap, *Weekenders* – during which someone died, another person was thrown out of their home, a wife cheated on her husband with the husband's best friend, and Aunty Ann put on about three kilos.)

... DURING A TRAUMATIC EPISODE OF HER FAVOURITE SOAP ...

'Mmmhamyum!' mumbles Uncle Nigel indistinctly, his mouth full. 'My favourite!'

'Don't talk with your mouth full, Nigel – especially not in front of Maddy!' snaps Aunty Ann.

(How old does she think I am?! It's not as if Uncle Nigel is performing a striptease – bleeee! BAD thought . . .)

'Sorry, Annie!'

Aunty Ann turns to me. 'So how was choir practice, Maddy?'

'It was *fine*!' I snarl.

Mum looks taken aback. 'Don't snap, Maddy, dear!'

'Sorry, Mum. Sorry, Aunty Ann.'

Aunty Ann picks a little piece of ham off her plate and places it on a smaller plate, pushing it along the table until it is just under Foofy's nose, who is sitting at the table on a kitchen stool, propped up with extra cushions so that he is at the right height. He sniffs at the ham, licks it, and then, without much enthusiasm, swallows it before leaning over to sniff at Aunty Ann's plate again.

I notice Mum wince – I know she hates having Foofy at the supper table. But she never says anything, because she doesn't want to upset Aunty Ann. Sometimes I think Mum is *too* nice . . .

'Anyone for Monopoly?' exclaims Uncle Nigel, after we have finished our peach melbas. Foofy is still chasing a slice of peach around his plate with his tongue – he can't get a grip on it . . . (I feel like shouting 'DOGS DON'T EAT PEACHES!!!' I also feel like shouting 'I HATE MONOPOLY!!!' But I don't. Rio really *would* shout something like that – and her parents would probably laugh . . . I wish I could go and see Rio . . .)

But any further musings are squeezed out of me as I sit sandwiched on the sofa between Aunty Ann with Foofy on her lap on one side and Uncle Nigel on the other. I feel myself sinking into a state not far removed from death through boredom. I have to keep pinching myself to make sure I am still alive.

'Are you OK, dear?' Mum enquires, following the most long-drawn-out Y-A-W-N that I have ever yawned.

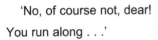

'I'm just tired, that's all. And I've got to get up early for my paper round tomorrow. Would you mind if I gave Monopoly a miss and went to bed?'

'No, of course not, dear! You run along . . .'

Run? I think not. I stagger up to my room and collapse on to some cushions on the floor, grabbing a nearby magazine (why are other people's lives so much more exciting than my own??!).

I set my alarm clock for . . . EARLY. VERY, VERY EARLY!

I must be mad, getting up like this on a Saturday – but the money I earn from my paper round is useful for buying magazines and stuff.

Scattering the village ducks in all directions, quacking loudly (they are ducks with a death wish and like to stand on one leg in the middle of the road), I pedal along the street on my trusty and now-going-rusty yellow bike, my eyes still bleary with sleep. Mr Ricketts walks past with his dog, Samson.

'Good morning, Maddy! You're up with the lark!'

(No, Mr Ricketts – you're wrong. The lark has more sense.

It is still in bed, snoring its head off. Or possibly it is extinct. Some people may blame chemical fertilisers, but I think it was the result of the lark's stupid habit of getting up too early . . .)

YAWN...

'Would you like your paper, Mr Ricketts? Or shall I deliver it to your house?'

EARLY...

'Oh, deliver it to the house, there's a good girl. Mrs Ricketts really looks forward to her *Daily Doom*.' (I bet!)

ZZZZ

Totally drained by too much early-morning cheerfulness (I do not *do* early-morning cheerfulness), I arrive back at the Village Stores at precisely the wrong moment.

THE LARK IS STILL IN BED, SNORING ITS HEAD OFF...

Mum staggers out of the door, carrying Mrs Ploughman's box of groceries to the car for her. Mrs Ploughman likes to do her shopping *early,* and I suspect that Mum, ever obliging, opens the shop early especially for her every Saturday. Sometimes I wish she'd speak her mind and tell Mrs Ploughman to do her shopping at a normal time. Instead she just complains to *me* when

12

'IT'S NO TROUBLE!'

MRS PLOUGHMAN

Mrs Ploughman isn't around – what good is *that*?!

Mrs Ploughman has seen me – it is too late!

'Maddy!' she exclaims. 'Goodness me – haven't you grown?' (She says this *every* Saturday. What does she expect me to do – *shrink*? I don't mean to have such grouchy thoughts, but I got up too early . . . I *know* that Mrs Ploughman means well . . .)

With a wan smile I turn to Mum and say: 'Is it OK if I go to Rio's now?' (I know that she won't be up yet, but I did this last Saturday and Rio let me crash out beside her on her double bed until we both felt that it was a *reasonable* time to get up – lunchtime.) 'I can take her parents their newspaper,' I add.

'Of course, darling!' says Mum. 'Have a nice time!'

'I will.'

The road slopes gently downhill from the Village Stores to Marsh Cottage at Bunbury Bottom, and I freewheel most of the way, enjoying the sensation of the air rushing past my

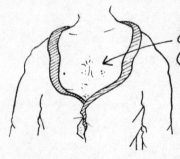

face, lifting my hair –

CHEST (FAINTLY HAIRY)

I am flying down to Rio!

The door of Marsh Cottage is opened by . . . Syd!!! He is wearing a dark blue towelling dressing gown – AND NOTHING UNDERNEATH!!! It is tied loosely – and I'm talking LOOSELY!!! Rio's big brother looks even more mouth-watering than usual – HELP! What if I start dribbling??! A kind of panic sweeps over me – I don't know what to say, what to do, where to look! All I can think is PHWOARGHHH coupled with an urge to leap on to my bike and pedal away very fast. (I feel myself getting very hot, and it is not just because of the heatwave we have had recently!) Syd is practically NAKED!!! WHERE am I meant to look??! I am far too embarrassed to look into his melting brown eyes (I mean they make *me* melt . . .), so I look at his chest (faintly hairy) and then at his legs (hairier than the chest). I close my eyes and feel myself swaying – am I about to pass out at his feet??! (Size eleven, I'd guess . . .)

FEET (SIZE ELEVEN, I WOULD GUESS – SWOOOOOOOOON...)

I half-open my eyes (what if the dressing gown has completely come undone? I'm only *half*-hoping that this has happened – it's OK – I'm not a *complete* perv!).

But Syd has wandered away into the house. 'Come in, Maddy!' he calls out casually, as if everything is normal (which I suppose, from his point of view, it is – but I don't think that I will ever feel normal again . . .). 'You'll find my little sister in her room, still snoring her head off. Mum and Dad are still in bed, too. But I've got some serious revision to get on with today – I've got non-stop exams at the moment. What's your excuse for being up so early?'

I open my mouth to say something, but instead of any intelligible sounds known to humankind, out comes this insane high-pitched giggle: 'HEE HEE HEE HEE HEE!!!' I close my mouth again. I want to DIE.

'Oh, well,' says Syd. 'I'll catch you later, Maddy.' He disappears off to his room.

Feeling like the most *uncool* thing in the entire universe, I trail sadly up the stairs and knock quietly on Rio's bedroom door. (Rio has painted her door pink and purple and daubed slogans on it such as 'School stinks!'. Mum would NEVER let me get away with anything like that! Doesn't Rio realise how lucky she is?)

'Come in!' Rio calls out sleepily. 'Hi, Maddy! It's too early. Let's snooze for a while . . .' she mutters, rolling over.

But I have never felt less like snoozing in my entire life. Lying on Rio's bed, staring fixedly at the glow-in-the-dark stars on her ceiling, my bottom lip begins to tremble and my eyes start to sting at the knowledge that I am terminally uncool, and

15

I WANT TO BE COOL!

that Syd must now think of me as a sad, giggling idiot.

'Maddy?'

'Yes?'

'I have never seen anyone look quite so tensed up as you're looking right now. You look like one of those city people when they first arrive at Mum and Dad's de-stressing place. Only worse.'

'Can I book myself in there – for the rest of my life?'

'No. You couldn't afford it.'

'SO WHAT AM I SUPPOSED TO DO?!'

'Maddy! Whatever is the matter?'

'Rio, do you and your family go to church?'

'What sort of question is that?'

'Just answer it.'

'OK – we don't. We're agnostic. We don't go to church, but we've got open minds. People are entitled to their beliefs. Live and let live. I could go on – do you want me to?'

'No . . . it's OK.' (The thing that was worrying me was the thought of singing in the choir at church on Sunday and then spotting Syd in the congregation. I couldn't bear it if he saw me wearing my red cassock – a sort of flowing red robe which makes me look like something you'd stick on top of the Christmas tree. A cassock is a *seriously* uncool garment – I can't believe I used to be *proud* of wearing it!)

'Maddy – you're being weird. What's wrong?'

'I saw your brother in his dressing gown.'

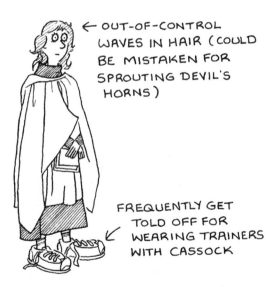

← OUT-OF-CONTROL WAVES IN HAIR (COULD BE MISTAKEN FOR SPROUTING DEVIL'S HORNS)

FREQUENTLY GET TOLD OFF FOR WEARING TRAINERS WITH CASSOCK

A CASSOCK IS A SERIOUSLY UNCOOL GARMENT . . .

'Oh, poor you! No wonder you're traumatised. Oh, no – don't tell me – you fancy him!'

'NO!!! I . . . I . . . I . . .'

'You fancy him. It's OK. Everyone does. I suppose he IS quite good-looking – in a brotherish sort of way. I fancy some of his mates.'

'Oh! I mean . . . do you? HEE HEE HEE HEE HEE . . .'

Rio is lying propped up on her elbow, her chin resting on her hand, giving me an 'oh-my-God-there's-no-hope-for-some-people' look.

'Rio?'

'Yes?'

'I want to be cool.'

Rio throws back her head, collapses on to her back and laughs loudly. 'Seriously?' she says, gulping down the laughter.

'Yes. Seriously cool.' (I don't say 'like you' – I have *some* pride!) 'Can you help me?'

'Well, I'm not the world's greatest authority on "cool",' says Rio. (That's what I like about her – she's cool without being big-headed.) 'I don't know.'

'PLEEEEEEASE!!! Ickle pretty please with heaps of sugar and an enormous genetically modified cherry on top?'

'OK, OK, I'll try!'

Chapter Three

Rio Rocks!

BOOM! BOOM! SHAKE DA ROOM!

It is Monday (no school as it is a staff training day – I hope they are training them to do something exciting such as jumping through flaming hoops, juggling with fire or building a human pyramid with Mr Cartridge-Penn the headmaster right on top!).

I am back at Rio's, and she has just put her stereo on – Big Sistaz and the Power of Sound Summer Groove (Remix). It is so heavy on bass that the walls start to vibrate and buzz. Stuff on Rio's shelves rattles, and a book falls off the end of one shelf. (Mum would *never* let me have my music turned up *this* loud!!! I wish Mum could be more like Rio's mum!)

'I'm into Urban!' shouts Rio over her music. 'Are you?'

'Yes!' (It makes a change from 'The Lord Is My Shepherd'.)

'I can't wait for the summer concert!' Rio yells. 'You know the group I've formed with Kate and Jaz – yeah? Well, Mr Crotchett has agreed to let us sing if we pass the audition. I forgot to tell you! So I'll be there at rehearsals, when you're doing your choir stuff!'

Rio's dad (he has short, cropped, fair hair and a short,

19

stubbly beard, and wears little round glasses) puts his head round the door – surely Rio's in for it now? I feel certain that her dad is about to have a go at her for turning the music up so loud.

Instead, he smiles at us pleasantly. 'Turn it up a bit, Rio!' he shouts. 'Mum and I are downstairs and we can't hear it properly – mind if I leave the door open? This music rocks, doesn't it?' He beams at us and departs, leaving Rio's bed-room door wide open.

My jaw sags. 'Wow!' I exclaim. 'Your parents are *so* COOL! They *like* your music! I wish Mum was cool. She'd make me turn it *down* so that we didn't upset the neighbours.'

'My parents are NOT cool!' snaps Rio. 'They're just annoying. It's this stupid reverse psychology thing – they're really into it, even though it doesn't work. They think that if they encourage me to turn my music up, I'll want to turn it down. Why do you want your mum to be cool, anyway? Parents aren't supposed to be cool – it's not a Parent Thing. I like your mum the way she is – she's really nice. She never has a bad word to say about anyone.'

'Hmmm . . . I'm not sure,' I muse. 'Sometimes she's nice to people's faces. Then, when they're not around, she says things. Your mum and dad are more upfront. You know where you are with them. They're really open. I wish Mum was.'

'Sometimes I wish they weren't so open – it can get embarrassing. Like when they draw everyone's attention to my latest piercing, and say "Isn't she brave?"'

'You're lucky!' I exclaim. 'I'm not even allowed to have my ears pierced a second time. And I want to be COOL!' I wail.

'Hey – stop stressing!' says Rio. 'I think you're pretty cool already.'

I smile. Rio is a good friend.

'But I'm not sure about your hair,' she continues.

'My hair? What's wrong with my hair?' I say defensively.

'Look – do you want my help, or not?'

'Sorry – carry on.'

'To be honest, your hair makes you look about twelve – but don't panic! I can help!'

Rio's dark hair has been cut into a dead-straight bob, with

I LOOK AS THOUGH I HAVE
A DEAD RODENT ON MY HEAD...

two long floppy strands of hair at the front, dangling either side of her face. One of these strands is longer than the other. She uses hair gel to spike up some shorter bits at the back. This is *seriously cool* hair.

I stare into a nearby mirror at my thatch of wavy hair. I look as though I have a dead rodent on my head.

Rio gets to work with her hair straightener, and by the time she has finished I do not recognise myself. I have perfectly straight hair! She has even given me two long floppy strands at the front.

'But you're not allowed to cut one of them shorter!' she warns me. 'That's *my* thing!'

'OK,' I say, grinning.

Rio lends me her old hair straightener (she has a new, improved one), and she says I can have some of her make-up – she has *loads*.

I DO NOT RECOGNISE
MYSELF...

(She even wears it to school, although we're not supposed to – somehow she gets away with it.) I choose a pink and purple

22

eyeshadow trio called EnergEYES, which Rio says she has never used – it didn't suit her – and some foundation and blusher. (Mum is reluctant to let me have make-up, although she did buy me a concealer stick for my spots. I tried using it on my lips in order to find out if it would work as a lipstick. It concealed my mouth, and the effect was very strange.)

My makeover is cut short by the arrival of Rio's dad again.

'Come along, Rio!' he says cheerfully. 'Time for the family powwow! Maddy can join in if she likes.'

'DAD! NO!!!'

'Come on, Rio! You know we have the powwow on Mondays now. And since you and Syd are both at home today, we can have it earlier than usual. See you downstairs in a few minutes, OK? Mum's just lighting the pipe of peace. Come on, you two! Let's POWWOW!'

'I . . . don't . . . think . . . so . . .' says Rio slowly, after her dad has gone downstairs again.

I am overcome with curiosity. 'Powwow?' I enquire.

'Oh, it's this stupid idea Mum and Dad came up with. We're supposed to sit in a circle and talk about stuff.'

'What stuff?'

'Any old stuff. Feelings and stuff.'

'And the pipe of peace?'

'It's a real native American peace pipe. But we don't smoke it or anything. Mum and Dad are anti-smoking – "Smoking pipes of peace kills!" and all that.'

'So why does your mum light it?'

'Oh, she sticks some incense in it and lights that. Then we

pass it around, and the person holding it is the one who talks.'

Rio's dad calls to us from the bottom of the stairs: 'Come on, Rio! We're waiting!'

'Oh, pants!' Rio groans. 'I suppose I won't get *any* peace until I get this over with. Let's go . . .'

'Er – did your dad say that Syd will be there, too?'

'Probably. He's more into this powwow thing than I am.'

'I . . . I'm not sure if . . .'

But there seems to be no escape – I am half-fascinated and half-terrified at the thought of sitting in a circle with Rio, her parents and Syd, talking about feelings and stuff . . . (I still think it's great that Rio's parents are so open, and I wish Mum would express her feelings and encourage me to express mine, instead of always being so nice and polite – at least to people's faces!)

Rio's mum greets us (she has long, dark hair and a lovely warm smile) and welcomes us into the living room. The curtains are drawn, and the room is lit by candles. The furniture has been moved back and cushions placed in a circle on the floor. (Rio's parents certainly go to a lot of trouble just to speak to their children . . .)

'Hi, Maddy!' Syd waves to me. He is already sitting cross-legged on a cushion, holding what must be the pipe of peace. It is a large carved and decorated pipe, with a few feathers tied to it and a wispy bit of smoke curling out of the bowl – the room smells of joss sticks. 'I like your hair, Maddy!' Syd calls out. (I am glad that the room is dark so that no one can see me blushing bright red – Syd is still in his dressing gown!)

When we are all sitting on our cushions (I am next to Syd!!!), Rio's dad says: 'Welcome to our powwow! And a special welcome to Maddy! The purpose of the powwow is to cleanse your spirit. You may talk freely about your feelings, and no one will be angry. We are here to listen, not to judge. Together we will find the way forward. Let's begin. May I have the pipe, Syd? Syd! May I have the pipe, please? Thank you. Please try to stay awake this time, Syd.'

Rio's dad starts the ball rolling by talking about the wonderful sense of togetherness which he is experiencing. Then he hands the pipe to me – my hands are trembling; I hope I don't drop it! I sit, holding the pipe. A clock ticks somewhere in the room. A fly buzzes. Syd pretends to snore.

'Be quiet, Syd!' says Rio's mum. 'Maddy, dear – how are you feeling?'

Total panic sets in – help! I *have* no feelings! All I am aware of is a great cloud of emptiness inside my head! (I feel very hot and experience a surge of resentment against Mum for not bringing me up to express my feelings, good or bad! When did Mum last ask me how I was feeling? I can't remember! And I can never be *quite* sure how she is feeling because of her infuriating tendency to hint at things instead of saying them openly.)

'Would you like some more time to think about it, dear?'

I nod. (Syd must still think of me as a total idiot – but at least I am a silent one this time instead of a giggling insane one.)

Rio's dad takes the pipe of peace and attempts to pass it to Rio. But Rio is sitting there, arms firmly folded and a face like thunder. Suddenly she explodes with anger and shouts that she *hates* this – she thinks it is totally weird and *really* embarrassing! Rio's dad nods and says: 'That's good. That's very good. You're saying what you really feel . . .'

With a loud shriek Rio leaps up and rushes out of the room. I follow her. It is a relief to get away, but I experience a fleeting sense of regret that I never got to find out what goes on inside Syd's head!

Rio makes me promise not to tell anyone at school how weird her parents are, and asks if she can come round to my place for a while. She lets me take the make-up she used on me.

We go into the Village Stores first to buy chocolate (we both feel in need of some serious comfort eating). Mrs Ploughman is in there, buying a jar of pickled onions. 'My, my, Maddy!' she exclaims. 'You've grown!'

'Yes – she's shooting up fast!' says Mum, counting out Mrs Ploughman's change. (And I'll be shooting out sideways too, after all this chocolate . . .)

Mum looks at me. 'You've done something to your hair, dear. It looks very . . . nice.' (Only Mum can make the word 'nice' sound like a criticism! I'd rather she didn't say anything

at all – why *pretend* to like my hair? I hate it when she says the opposite of what she means.)

'What happened to all those lovely curls?' Mrs Ploughman asks. 'So angelic!'

I ask Mum if Rio and I can go up to my room for a while. As we go through the door at the back of the shop, which leads to the stairs up to our flat (there is also a door leading out into a small garden), I overhear Mum saying to Mrs Ploughman: 'I *did* think it was good for Maddy, having a friend of her own age in the village . . .' I glance back over my shoulder and notice that Mum and Mrs Ploughman are leaning towards each other over the counter and talking in a confidential manner – why?

But Rio is calling me, so I keep going up the stairs . . .

Later on, after Rio has gone home, Mum confiscates the make-up that Rio lent me, saying that it is not hypo-allergenic and will bring me out in spots. 'You can give it back to Rio when you next see her,' says Mum.

'Rio doesn't want it back. So can I have it?' I reply.

'No, darling. Either give it back to Rio or I'm throwing it away. You can't wear it to school, anyway.'

'Rio wears make-up to school.'

'Well, she shouldn't.'

'But she does.'

'Her parents should stop her.'

'*Her* parents don't mind.'

'Maddy . . .'

'Don't you like Rio?'

Mum looks surprised. 'Of course I do, darling. I'm only concerned about the effect she might be having on you. And I'm a little worried about that brother of hers . . . He comes into the shop sometimes.'

'Syd?'

'Is that his name? He looks as if he never bothers to brush his hair . . .'

(WHAT?! Syd has *the* most sexy messed-up hair in the world! What can Mum possibly have against his hair?)

'I . . . I like his hair!'

'That's OK, dear. But I'm not very keen on that ring through his eyebrow. And I don't like his trousers.'

'It's OK, Mum. Syd's really nice. And what have you got against his trousers?'

'Too many pockets. Makes you wonder what he keeps in

'I DON'T LIKE HIS TROUSERS...'

them. And the crotch is where a boy's knees used to be in my day.'

Mum looks straight at me. 'I don't mind you being friends with Rio, darling – although I don't think you should let her do your hair again. And don't copy the way she dresses – that skirt she wears is far too short. I'm surprised her mother lets her out of the house looking like that! Not much parental control or direction in that household, I would imagine. Her parents are . . . alternative, aren't they?'

'They're cool. So's Rio. So's Syd.' (It's so annoying, the way Mum criticises people behind their backs just because they're different from her – and she doesn't even know them!)

'Yes, darling – of course. I don't mean to upset you. But when I told you that you had better do your homework in time for school tomorrow, I didn't like the way Rio shouted "Homework should be banned!" And when I went out of the room, I thought I heard her say something else about home-

work which sounded quite rude. I hope she isn't allowed to use words like that at home.'

I shrug. 'She was just being Rio . . .'

'OK, dear. I also know that you're a sensible girl who would never do anything that *you* know isn't right.'

I fume silently (I do a lot of silent fuming these days). Is Mum implying that Rio is the sort of girl who *would* do something that wasn't right? But, as usual, Mum has said it so nicely, smiling at me, her head tilted slightly to one side. It is hard for me to argue. (*Rio* seems to find it easy to argue!)

Mum leans forward to give me a hug. 'I love you, Maddy. Sorry if I've offended you. I just get a bit worried.'

'I love you too, Mum. It's OK. I understand.' (With a massive effort I have swallowed down my anger – Rio would have let rip!)

Mum sniffs the air. 'What's that smokey smell? It's coming from your hair, Maddy.'

'Oh, that's nothing. We were just passing the pipe of peace. It's OK, Mum – we didn't smoke it . . .'

The expression on Mum's face says it all – *now* I'm in for it . . .

Half an hour later . . .

After my lengthy explanation, Mum finally accepts – although she still looks suspicious – that Rio's parents do not encourage young people to smoke. With a final parting shot that she would prefer it if I didn't spend *quite* so much time with Rio and her family, she leaves me to finish my homework, have supper and get to bed. As my mind drifts gently downstream into sleep, I wonder how Mum would react if I were to daub slogans on my bedroom door: 'School stinks!' and 'Rio rocks!

Chapter Four

Tuesday Morning
Blues (and Greens . . .)

'IS IT something I said, Maddy?' Rio asks, staring at my contorted features.

'No! It's nothing you said! I'm looking like this because I suffer from bus sickness . . .'

The old school bus gives an extra-large lurch and I clap my hand over my mouth. Rio quickly moves to another seat just across the aisle, at a safe distance (or that's what she thinks. Hasn't she heard of projectile vomiting? Uuuurgh . . . Must try to think of something to take my mind off feeling sick . . .).

'They ought to provide sick bags,' Rio remarks helpfully. 'I expect they used to, but it's probably part of a cutback to save money and resources. No more sick bags. I suppose they could recycle them. Actually, that's a really bad thought . . . Fancy being sick into a bag which already has bits of somebody else's sick in it . . .'

'RIO! SHUT UP!!!'

'Sorry. You're not usually as bad as this.'

'I know. Mum's been seriously winding me up. She won't let me wear that make-up you gave me . . .'

BUS SICKNESS

'Oh, no wonder you look all pale and washed-out!' says Rio. 'You need a bit of colour, girl!'

'Mum says I've got to give the make-up back to you. But she's hidden it somewhere, so I can't. And I didn't get my Food Technology homework finished, so Miss Lemongrass is going to go majorly mad, and I'll probably get a detention . . .'

'Oh, you mean that project on sauces? Mine went all thick and yellow and lumpy. It looked like . . . er, sorry!'

An empty crisp packet sails over my head. Rio picks it up and hurls it back.

'Gotcha!' she shouts. 'Right between the eyes!' Some boys sitting right at the back start laughing (Rio and I are three rows from the back). I know that one of the boys is Syd, but I don't want to turn round and ogle him because: a) it would be a bit obvious (like wearing a hat with a flashing sign on top, saying: 'I FANCY YOU!'), and b) I don't want him to see me looking the same colour as a pea, or run the risk of doing some serious projectile vomiting which would effectively mean that neither Syd nor any of the other boys would ever come within a hundred yards of me again – at least not without full protective clothing – and my chances of a romantic encounter with any of them would be reduced to nil. (Not that my chances are much more than nil at the moment . . .)

'Maddy?' Rio is looking at me nervously. 'Are you OK?'

'No. I need something to take my mind off the fact that I am in a hot, noisy, crowded bus with tartan seats the same colour as puke . . .'

'Here – look at this!' Rio thrusts a folded piece of paper into my hand. 'I wrote down some tips for you. I wanted to e-mail them, but then I remembered that you . . . don't . . . have . . . a . . . computer . . .'

Rio speaks the words slowly in the same way that she might say: 'I remembered that you don't have a navel . . .', as she seems to equate not having a computer with being a kind of alien being. At least, if I was an alien and really didn't have a navel, it would explain why I hadn't had it pierced, and it would be a cooler and more original explanation than the real one, which is 'Mum won't let me', Rio has had *her* navel pierced *three* times! But my mind is wandering . . . Rio is staring at me . . .

'Can't you persuade your mum to get a computer?' she asks (not for the first time since we met several months ago).

'I already told you ages ago – she doesn't like them. And she says she can't afford one. But mainly she doesn't like them. She doesn't want me to have access to the Internet – she's worried that I might log on to a dodgy chat room . . .'

'Doesn't she trust you at all?'

'I don't know . . . I think she's just scared that something bad might happen to me . . .'

Rio shakes her head sadly. 'Didn't you say nearly a week ago that you might be able to e-mail me off your uncle's computer? Have you asked him yet?'

'No – but I will.'

Rio looks thoughtful. 'So the bottom line is: you don't have a computer, you don't have a mobile phone, and you haven't had your navel pierced.'

I nod, feeling greener than ever.

'Maddy, we *seriously* need to bring you out of the Dark Ages!' says Rio. 'At least we've got your hair sorted – you've done a good job with the hair straightener, by the way. Now you need to read *that*!' She points to the folded piece of paper, which I am still clutching in my hand. Unwillingly (reading in a moving vehicle tends to make the sick feeling worse, but I don't like to refuse Rio's offer of help), I unfold the piece of paper, and read:

HOW TO BE COOL
by Rio de Havilland

a) Avoid wearing anything which gets the following reaction from your parent:

- 'That's nice, dear.'
- 'It's lovely to see you looking like a girl for a change.'
- 'Your grandparents would approve of that.'
- 'Now *those* are what I call *sensible* shoes . . .'

b) Try to look bored, even if *the* most delectable and ohmygod beautiful boy in the world has just walked into the room. You want him to notice you because you're cool, and not because you're the grinning, drooling idiot prostrating herself at his feet.

'NOW THOSE ARE WHAT I CALL SENSIBLE SHOES...'

c) Get into cool, hip music such as rap or urban. Be able to talk about it but don't get boring. Swap CDs.

'That's as far as I got,' says Rio. 'Oh, come on – it's not *that* bad! At least I tried – I even made it funny. You look like it's the worst thing, like you've just read your own death sentence . . .'

'I *told* you, Rio – I'm feeling SICK! Reading has made it worse – it's nothing to do with what you wrote. That's fine, thank you. Now just let me die.'

I lean back and close my eyes. Thankfully, the journey is nearly over. Soon we are jostling to get off the bus, getting hit (accidentally) by backpacks as people hoist them on to their shoulders. It is good to feel solid ground beneath my feet, and I take some deep breaths.

As we head across the car park to the main entrance, Rio shoves a CD into the side pocket of my bag.

'What's that?'

'It's an old M Power wiv MC Fatarse CD that I don't want any more. Go and swap it with someone you fancy at lunch-break, or something.'

'But . . . but what if they don't have a CD to give me in exchange?'

'Well, they can *owe* you! For heaven's sake, girl – you don't half get bogged down in details. Oh, there's Kate and Jaz! I've got to speak to them about the concert. See you at the lunchtime rehearsal! We're auditioning today – I'm reeeeally nervous! So I'll see you there, and you can tell me how you got on with the CD . . .'

M POWER WIV M C FATARSE

38

HANNAH, RACHEL AND DAISY
(THE SLIGHTLY-LESS-COOL CROWD)

'Yes, but . . . there won't be much time . . . we've got to be in the hall by quarter past . . .' Too late. Rio is chatting excitedly with Kate and Jaz (they are in the same class for most lessons), and I know I won't see much of her until the journey home again. I feel a surge of jealousy – Rio seems to find it so easy to be one of the Cool Crowd, while I am a fully paid-up member of the Slightly-Less-Cool Crowd –

KATE AND JAZ

alas! It's not that I don't like them – we all went to the same primary school – Hannah, Rachel, Daisy and me. We get on well – they're nice and kind and funny. Hannah sneezes *really* loudly, and she made the whole class laugh once by doing this when Mr Edmondson (who teaches maths) had just asked for quiet. That's the sort of wild and wacky behaviour the Slightly-Less-Cool-Crowd goes in for . . .

But I can't help it – I would really *like* to hang out with the cool people more (especially now that I have cool hair! I even get up half an hour earlier every morning to straighten it before school. I have bags under my eyes, but it's worth it – I think. Hannah, Rachel and Daisy have all said how much they like my new hairstyle. I just hope that I can keep it looking good – and stay awake!)

I am going to have to move fast if I want to swap a CD with someone hunky before the rehearsal *and* eat my sandwiches (I'm no longer feeling sick – what a relief! – and I'm *starving*!). I can't help feeling that being in a tearing hurry is probably *un*cool – but I don't have time to worry about this! Scoffing down a ham sandwich, I bolt into the girls' toilets for a pee and to check my appearance in a mirror. This is a mistake, as any remaining shred of confidence I may have had disappears as I look at my shiny, un-made-up face (*why* did Mum have to confiscate and then *hide* that make-up?!), and my *hair*. It is still straight on one side, but on the other side I obviously didn't straighten it enough, and it has reverted *completely* to how it used to be. It's gone all wavy and is sort of sticking out sideways. I splash water on my hand and attempt to flatten it down. Now I look as though half of me has just been swimming! I can't face anyone looking like this! But I don't want to let Rio down . . .

IT IS STICKING OUT
SIDEWAYS...

40

Emerging from the girls' toilets, I see Syd and his friends walking towards me down the corridor – it is now or never!

'Hi, Syd!' I call out breathlessly. (I immediately realise that this sounds far too enthusiastic, so I attempt to look bored.)

NOW I LOOK AS THOUGH HALF OF ME HAS BEEN SWIMMING ...

'Maddy,' he mutters as he walks past with his mates. (I hear one of them say, 'Who's that?' and Syd replies, 'Oh, just a friend of my kid sister.')

Hang on! I haven't swapped that CD yet!

'Syd!' I call after him.

Syd turns round and gives me a bored look. (OK – don't worry! He's not really bored – he's just being cool.) 'What is it?' he asks.

My mind goes blank. Syd and his friends are all looking at me. After the longest few seconds I have ever experienced, I remember the CD! I suppose I can't really swap one of Rio's CDs with her own brother – and she'd laugh at me again! But his friends are quite hunky, too . . . 'Would any of you like to swap a CD?' I ask squeakily.

'What CD?' asks a friend with bleached blond hair.

Total panic sets in – I can't remember!

Fumbling feverishly in my bag – oh, where *is* it?! Of course, it's in the side pocket, but it's caught on a thread – it won't come out!

'Er . . . er . . . er . . .' I stammer. 'Er . . . er . . . Erban!!!'

'Erban?'

'Yes! You know – FATARSE!'

'Who are you calling "Fat arse"?' shouts blondie.

'No! I mean . . .' I stutter.

'Fat arse yourself!' he shouts back at me. And they all walk away, laughing (reducing my chances of a romantic encounter with any of them to minus nil. My life is in ruins!)

Hannah, Rachel and Daisy have just joined me and are looking at me with a certain amount of respect.

'Did you just call one of those boys "Fat arse"?' whispers Daisy. (I get the impression that 'fat arse' are not words that she has ever used in her life before . . .)

'Sort of . . .' I reply, trying not to look as miserable as I feel.

'Cool!' they chorus.

'We'd better hurry,' says Hannah, looking at her watch, 'or we'll be late for the rehearsal, and Mr Crotchett will go mad.'

'Mr Crotchett *is* mad,' I remark, rallying slightly at the thought of the concert – I enjoy concerts. 'But we'd better not be late.' (Then I remember that Rio and the rest of the Cool Crowd are fashionably late for nearly everything and slow my pace.)

At the rehearsal

The hall is full of people tuning their instruments and planning their performances for the summer concert, which is taking place on Wednesday evening next week. (Goodness knows how Rio managed to persuade Mr Crotchett to let her take part at this late stage – the rest of us have been practising for *months*, since before Rio even joined the school! But she still has the final audition to come . . .)

Hannah, Rachel and I are all in the choir, and we are singing a selection of sea shanties – cool, eh? I realise with a sinking sensation that if Rio is performing in the concert, it is possible that Syd may be in the audience, and he will hear all my 'Yo-ho-hoing' and 'Heave-ho, me hearties!' Worse still, Mr Crotchett wants me to give a solo rendition of 'Who will have the fishy, on the little dishy, who will have the fishy, when the bo-at comes in'. Now I am feeling sick again – I shouldn't have swallowed that ham sandwich whole. I think I'm feeling seasick . . .

FISHY ON A DISHY

Daisy plays the oboe in the orchestra, which will be accompanying the choir when we sing our sea shanties. Daisy will also be doing a solo piece on the oboe, and there are one or two other solo performances lined up, as well as a session from Mr Wheatengreen's jazz group. (Mr Wheatengreen teaches geography, but his main passion in life is the jazz group.) The rest of the performances will be by various student bands, mostly Year Elevens (Syd's year) or Sixth Formers – the notable exception being Rio and her friends.

'Hi, Maddy!' It's Rio.

'Hello!'

'So how did it go? Did you swap a CD with a handsome hunk?' she asks.

'No. But I tried.'

'Oh, well! Better luck next time! Who was he?'

'Dunno. He had bleached hair. He was with Syd.'

'Oh . . . I think I know him – was he taller than Syd, with quite a thin face?'

'Yes.'

'That was Matt, Syd's friend! He's cool!'

'I called him a fat arse.'

But before Rio can say anything (I am on the receiving end of an 'are-you-COMPLETELY-mad?' look . . .), Mr Crotchett calls for our attention – it is the choir's turn to practise first. I get to do my 'little squishy fishy on a dishy' thing, and Mr Crotchett gets angry because he says I am not putting enough 'oomph' into it – this is because I keep imagining an audience with Syd and Matt and Syd's other friends all sitting in the front row and pointing and laughing at me . . . I tell Mr Crotchett that I am not feeling well.

Rio, Kate and Jaz are calling themselves 'Sistaz of Shame'. Kate plays the guitar and Rio has persuaded a few of the year elevens who play guitar and drums to be their backing group. (How does she do it?) They are about to audition a number that Rio has told Mr Crotchett she really wants to perform.

When the Sistaz of Shame have finished belting out the number, which has only one lyric which goes 'EM-EM-EM-EM-EM-EM-MUSIC-SICK-SICK-SICK-SICK-SICK-SICK' over and over again, there is a profound silence in the hall. Everyone looks at Mr Crotchett, holds their breath and waits for his reaction. (He has been sitting on a chair throughout the performance with his head in his hands.) He rises to his feet a little unsteadily and says, 'That was quite stunningly *awful*.' (Nervous laughter all round . . .) 'But,' he continues, 'I think it is probably time to break new ground at St Swithin's, and it was certainly *different* – so I am going to stick my neck out, and keep it in! I may live to regret this,' he adds, as Rio, Kate and Jaz squeal with delight and hug each other.

For a moment I think that Rio is going to hug Mr Crotchett as well, but she rushes over to me instead with a cry of 'Isn't it great, Maddy? Now we're *both* going to be in the concert!'

(And your brother's probably going to be in the audience . . .)

'Great!' I exclaim, with as much enthusiasm as I can muster.

When the rehearsal is over, Mr Crotchett tells us that the dress rehearsal will be on Monday next week.

'Members of the choir – please remember to bring stripy jerseys or T-shirts and three-quarter-length trousers – or bell-bottoms, if you've got them! No eyepatches or stuffed parrots, please. Thank you – goodbye.'

In my bedroom, with Rio (I survived the bus journey home – just . . .)

'What are bell-bottoms?' I ask, kicking off my school shoes – and then picking them up and putting them neatly beside my bed.

'Another name for flares,' says Rio. 'Serious flares. *Some* people like them, including Dad – he's got a pair. They're

45

DAD'S GOT A PAIR — FROM HIS PSYCHEDELIC PHASE — HE'S *SO* EMBARRASSING!

green and yellow stripes and made of corduroy. They're from his psychedelic phase. He's *so* embarrassing . . .'

'Don't say that! He's really nice. You're lucky. I don't even *have* a dad.' (I didn't mean to react like this – I guess I'm just super-sensitive on the subject of dads.)

'Oh, sorry.' Rio looks uncomfortable.

'No, *I'm* sorry. I didn't mean to have a go at you. I've had a total pants sort of day. And I'm talking serious *flared* pants!

MY LIFE IS TOTAL 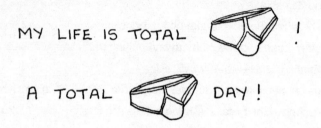 !

A TOTAL 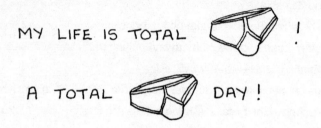 DAY !

But I'm really pleased for you – about being in the concert, I mean!'

'Yes, it's great, isn't it?'

'There's just one thing . . .'

'What? Didn't you like the song?'

'No, the song's . . . great. Just tell me that Syd's busy that night and won't be able to come to the concert . . .'

'Why should I tell you *that*? I *want* Syd to be there. And Mum and Dad will be there, I expect, doing the whole proud parent thing. Just wait until you see what Kate, Jaz and I are going to be wearing – you ain't seen nothin' yet! Don't worry about Syd – he's cool. Tell you one thing, though, Maddy . . .'

'What?'

'Your room is worryingly tidy. It's uncool to be this tidy. I tidy my room twice a year – once before my birthday and once on Christmas Eve – to make room for all the new stuff.' She yawns. 'Well, I must be going. See you bright and early on the bus tomorrow. Have you thought about self-hypnosis to help with the bus-sickness? Just keep saying to yourself, "I do not get bus-sick, I do not get bus-sick, I do not get bus-sick . . ."'

After Rio has gone, the flat seems very quiet. Mum must still be downstairs in the shop . . . I wonder where she's hidden that make-up? I hope she hasn't thrown it away! Feeling guilty (but why? Rio gave that make-up to *me*, and Mum had no right to take it!), I conduct a search

ENERGEYES
11

which eventually leads me to a high shelf where Mum keeps the medicines. There, right at the back, behind the cold remedies and the wart remover, is my make-up! I grab it, replacing the cold remedies and wart remover carefully so that Mum won't notice that anything has been moved, and hurry back to my room, where I stuff the make-up under my mattress. Now I feel downright *bad*.

Thinking that I may as well do 'bad' properly, I decide to put on the CD that Rio gave me. Soon the relentless techno thumping beat of M Power wiv MC Fatarse is reverberating through the flat, making the pictures on the walls rattle . . .

'MADDY!' shouts Mum, who has suddenly burst through the door from the shop, followed by an out-of-breath Aunty Ann, wobbling badly and carrying an even more out-of-breath Foofy. 'What on *earth* is that NOISE?! Turn it OFF! It nearly gave poor Mrs Partridge a heart attack – she only came in for a packet of Rich Tea biscuits and suddenly there was this booming noise over our heads – she thought it was the Blitz all over again!'

'Sorry, Mum.' I have stopped the music.

'And what I heard of the lyrics was quite obscene!' Mum exclaims.

'It does say "Parental Advisory" on the cover – I think that means that parents are advised to leave the room when it's on.'

'Maddy! This isn't a joking matter! I'm confiscating that CD.'

'You can't! It's Rio's!' (What is Mum's problem? I think she wants to confiscate my LIFE!!!)

'Ah, that explains a lot!' says Aunty Ann, knowingly. 'I told you that you were letting Maddy see too much of that young lady, Helen. She's leading Maddy astray, I'm afraid.'

I feel like shouting, 'What do *you* know, you silly old jelly!' But I content myself with glaring at Aunty Ann.

'Don't glare at your aunt, Maddy!'

'Is the bad girl frightening poor Foofy-Woofy?' coos Aunty Ann, stroking Foofy.

I am *not* a bad girl!

Or perhaps I am . . .

'Hand over the CD, please, Maddy. There's a good girl. We'll talk about this another time. I need to close the shop and get tea ready – and I should probably send a post-traumatic stress counsellor round to see Mrs Partridge . . .'

Chapter Five

Crap at Cricket

'MADDEEEEEEEEEE! It's meeeeeeeee!'

Rio's friendly cry breaks the stillness of a hot Sunday afternoon (following on from a hot four days at school last week, and an equally hot Saturday – the heatwave shows no sign of ending). Rio is running towards me across the village green, smiling and waving. (She can be cool *and* friendly at the same time, unlike Syd's friends!)

'Hi, Rio!' (I find myself looking around uneasily, in case Mum is hiding in the bushes somewhere, watching me. Knowing that she doesn't like Rio makes me feel uneasy, although I know I shouldn't let her opinions bother me. Perhaps I should just be open about this with Rio.)

'Hi, Maddy! Are you OK? You seem a bit . . . I don't know. Not like your usual self.'

'Er . . . Mum's not very happy about us hanging out together at the moment, that's all. She's worried that . . . that . . .'

'I'm a bad influence?'

'Something like that.'

'Flattered, I'm sure!' (But Rio doesn't look flattered. She

50

looks hurt.) 'That fits with what you told me about having to give the make-up back. I don't *want* it back, by the way.'

'It's OK – I found it on a shelf, and I've stuffed it under my mattress. Mum doesn't know. And listen – don't worry! I'm not going to stop seeing you because of Mum. She can't stop me seeing who . . . who I like!'

'Good for you!' says Rio, grinning. 'I think you're pretty cool. But I really thought your mum liked me. She was always so nice . . .' Rio looks sad. 'It explains why she said you weren't coming out, when I came round to your place yesterday. She said you were tired and needed a rest. And I've hardly seen anything of you all week. I've been too busy practising for the concert with Kate and Jaz.' (I'd noticed – and I've tried not to care that Rio doesn't seem to have time for me, even after school, but I suppose it's because of the concert. And now I feel sorry for her, because of Mum . . .)

'Don't look now,' I mutter, welcoming an opportunity to change the subject, 'but here comes Aunty Ann with Foofy on the lead – or is it Uncle Nigel on the lead? No, it's Foofy – and she's heading our way . . .'

It is too late to escape. There is a sound of puffing and panting, wheezing and gasping – it is hard to know who's panting more heavily, Foofy or Aunty Ann.

Aunty Ann bends down and picks up Foofy. 'Poor little scrap!' she gasps. 'Shall Mummy carry her iddums-diddums dog?' (She kisses Foofy on the nose – YEURGH! – there's no telling where that nose has been! Foofy's nose is like a dirt-seeking missile, drawn to all things vile and disgusting . . .)

Aunty Ann gives Rio a strongly disapproving look and turns her back on her.

'I *won't* tell your mother that you have been going against my advice and talking to this young lady, but only if I see you at the cricket match, which is due to start in half an hour. I expect you to join in the cheers and applause for Nigel, who will be opening the batting. Your mother will be there, too,' she whispers.

Aunty Ann sniffs loudly and walks away, throwing us a final distrustful bulging-eyed look over her shoulder . . .

Uncle Nigel strides purposefully on to the village green, resplendent in his cricket whites, to a small burst of applause from the dozen or so villagers, including Mum, Aunty Ann and myself, who have dutifully turned out to see the Little Bunbury first eleven lose, as usual, to the Long Bunbury team. (Uncle Nigel usually hits the ball into the Wee, and someone has to roll up their trousers and go and fetch it.)

Uncle Nigel acknowledges the applause by waving his bat in the air, and Aunty Ann shouts, 'Hurrah!'

I am sitting on a bench between Mum and Aunty Ann, and there is little chance of escape. Rio is lurking just behind the pavilion, which is just to the right of where we are sitting, and whenever I look round she pulls a face at me.

'Concentrate, Maddy!' hisses Aunty Ann. 'You might miss something.' (Yes – someone might actually *move*. Cricket has to be *the* most *boring* game!)

The Long Bunbury Fast Bowler begins his run-up, gathers speed (it would be exciting if he took off – the Amazing Flying Cricketer!), takes aim and bowls overarm at Uncle Nigel.

Uncle Nigel wallops it. But this time he doesn't wallop it into

MUM FAILS TO MOVE IN TIME . . .

the Wee. The ball sails high into the air over our heads and then drops . . . AAAARGH! I dive sideways, Aunty Ann falls off the bench backwards, legs in the air (an unlovely sight), but Mum fails to move in time – the ball hits her right on top of the head.

'MUM!!!'

Mum collapses, quite slowly and gracefully (unlike Aunty Ann, who fell like a sack of potatoes in jelly), sideways on to the bench. Mrs MacGregor-Willey, who is a qualified first-aider as well as being in charge of the refreshment tent, rushes over with her first-aid pack – but Mum is already coming round.

'Wh . . . wh . . . what happened?' she asks in a faraway voice.

'It's OK, Mum – it's going to be OK!' I tell her. (I am REALLY scared – but I try to stay calm, for Mum's sake.)

'I'm so sorry, Helen – I'm so sorry!' Uncle Nigel has come racing over. He looks very upset.

'Someone ought to get her to the hospital for an X-ray,' says Mrs MacGregor-Willey, 'in case the skull is fractured. Don't worry, dear,' she says to me kindly. 'Your mum will be OK. Try to keep her awake, won't you?'

Rio has come over and puts a comforting arm around my shoulders. (I am so glad she's there – I feel very shaky . . .)

'I'll take her straight to casualty,' says Uncle Nigel. 'I'm sure you can spare me, can't you?'

'Perhaps we ought to abandon the match,' says Mrs MacGregor-Willey. 'We could just have tea instead.'

'Nnnno,' murmurs Mum. 'You carry on. I'll be OK with Nnnnigel. And Maddy.'

Suddenly a muffled voice behind us says: 'Will someone *please* help me up?' It is Aunty Ann, who is still upside down with her legs in the air, partly smothered by her own floral dress and lacy petticoats.

About six hours later we are back from the hospital. (Rio went home before we went to the hospital and told me to call her and tell her what happened – I managed to call her from the hospital.) Mum has had her head X-rayed, and fortunately no serious damage seems to have been done. But she has a bump on her head the size of a golf ball and is now sitting in front of the telly, a family-size packet of frozen peas on top of her head, watching *Weekenders*. Aunty Ann is fussing around, plumping cushions and wittering on about Uncle Nigel's brilliant batting and how unfortunate it was that Mum happened to be sitting in the wrong place.

'Oh, will you SHUT UP, Ann!' says Mum, suddenly.

Aunty Ann freezes mid-cushion-plump, her mouth open, halfway through saying the word 'Nige . . .' For a few seconds not a single part of her wobbles – she has turned into a petrified jelly! Then she comes to life again and starts wobbling so convulsively that I think that she is either going to explode and send jelly bits flying into all corners of the room or she is about to burst into tears. (Either of these things would not be good.)

I am pretty shocked, too. I don't think that I have *ever* heard

Mum tell *anyone* to 'shut up' before! The closest she gets is, 'Please be quiet'. She didn't even say, 'Shut up, *please!*'

'Oh, dear me! Oh, dear me!' babbles Aunty Ann. 'I'm sure I didn't mean to upset you, Helen – it's been a very trying day for all of us!'

'RUBBISH! All *you've* done is think about yourself as usual!' Mum exclaims. 'I'm the one sitting here with an enormous bump and a packet of frozen peas on my head!'

'I . . . I think I'll go and help Nigel in the kitchen!' says Aunty Ann in a shaky voice. 'Supper must be nearly ready.' She wobbles off into the kitchen.

(I feel a strange mixture of horror and delight at what has just happened . . . At *last* Mum has put Aunty Ann in her place! It's just so weird!!! But I expect it's just because Mum is majorly stressed after such a horrible day – I'm sure she'll be apologising to Aunty Ann like mad before too long.)

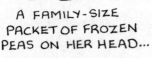

A FAMILY-SIZE PACKET OF FROZEN PEAS ON HER HEAD...

Mum approaches the supper table with a look on her face which none of us are used to seeing. She looks . . . cross.

'I like the way you're balancing those frozen peas on your head, Helen!' exclaims Uncle Nigel jovially. 'Just like they do in African countries!'

'I think you'll find that they balance baskets of fruit and vegetables, Nigel, *not* frozen peas! And I have a thumping headache, so I hardly think that it's a joking matter, especially since it's all *your* fault. You're crap at cricket!'

(Wow! That was *so* rude!!!)

There is a stunned silence. A dying fly buzzes on the windowsill, spinning in circles on its back. Then it stops. Aunty Ann is quivering all over. I have *never* heard Mum say the word 'crap' before – it is not a Mum word. The Cool Crowd at school use words like that! (Has Mum suddenly become cool?!)

'Nigel . . . !' gasps Aunty Ann. 'Nigel . . . is . . . (puff, pant, wheeze) BRILLIANT . . . at . . . CRICKET!'

Mum rolls her eyes, sits back in her chair, folds her arms and says 'sure' in a sarcastic manner. (This is seriously weird un-Mum-like behaviour . . . I am in shock, sitting with my mouth hanging open . . .)

'No, Helen's right,' says Uncle Nigel sadly. 'I'm not very good at cricket. And I am *so* sorry about the accident.' He looks upset. Mum smiles wanly at him. 'It's OK, Nigel,' she says.

Encouraged, Uncle Nigel indicates the food laid out on the table. 'Please eat something, Helen,' he says. 'You must keep your strength up. Look – I've prepared your favourite meal – ham, salad and boiled potatoes . . .'

'*Your* favourite, you mean, Nigel!' Mum erupts. '*Every*

Friday I prepare that meal, especially for you. It is *so* BORING! Boring, boring, boring, BORING!'

Silence again. (I feel like cheering. I wholeheartedly agree with Mum about the boringness of Uncle Nigel's favourite meal. Then I notice the devastated look on Uncle Nigel's face, and I feel sorry for him – he doesn't really deserve this!)

'What I'd really like,' Mum continues, 'is a curry. A really *hot* one!'

'Oh, I can't tolerate spicy foods,' says Aunty Ann. 'They bring me out in a hot flush.'

'We weren't talking about *you*!' snaps Mum fiercely. Aunty Ann wobbles violently. (Go, Mum!)

'And do we *have* to have that . . . that ANIMAL sitting at the supper table with us?' shouts Mum, pointing at Foofy, who is nibbling delicately at a piece of ham which he has just thieved from Aunty Ann's plate.

This is too much for Aunty Ann. No one calls her beloved Foofy-Woofy, iddums-diddums-dog, darling precious huggums 'n' Squeezums an ANIMAL!!!

'Come on, Nigel!' she barks, scooping Foofy up in her arms. 'I can tell that we're not welcome here! I think we'd better leave.' She marches out. (I feel like shouting 'YAY!' and punching the air with my fist – or, at least, politely applauding . . . although I still feel a bit sorry for Uncle Nigel.)

Uncle Nigel gets up to leave. He looks worried.

'You must take it easy, Helen,' he says. 'You're bound to feel not quite yourself after a nasty bang on the head like that. I expect you'll feel better by the morning. You . . . you know where I am, Maddy,' he says in a low voice, leaning close to me. 'If you need help. Call me immediately. Your mum's a bit out of sorts because she's got a bad headache – but she's going to be fine. Try not to worry.'

'*Kindly* do not talk about me as if I'm not here, Nigel!' says Mum. 'My hearing is as good as it ever was.'

'Sorry, Helen. I'll . . . I'll come back in the morning . . .'

I don't want Uncle Nigel to leave. I feel uneasy about being left alone with a mum who is behaving so weirdly, even though I thoroughly enjoyed seeing her put Aunty Ann in her place. But I'm worried about who she might have a go at next . . . me? I smile at her nervously. Apart from the packet of frozen peas on her head, she looks quite normal. She even smiles back at me!

'Don't worry about the washing-up, darling – you must do your homework and get to bed. I'll be fine – I feel better already now that *she's* gone!' (I take it that she means Aunty Ann – I never realised that Mum disliked her so much!)

I seize the opportunity to escape to my room (never before has maths homework seemed so attractive!), after telling Mum to call me if she needs anything.

'You're a lovely girl, Maddy!' says Mum. 'I love you.'

'Love you too, Mum.' (Phew! I think she's getting back to normal . . .)

Chapter Six

Thongs and Things

'MADDY! Are you wearing make-up?'

'It's . . . it's for the school concert, Mum – it's the dress rehearsal today. Mr Crotchett told us to dress up and wear make-up. We're supposed to be sailors – and sailors wear make-up. It's a well-known fact. Sorry, Mum – I've got to go!'

I make my escape before Mum can ask any more questions about make-up – or say anything weird. I think she's back to normal, although I wouldn't mind if she went on speaking her mind to Aunty Ann. I can't wait to tell Rio . . .

On the bus

'She said *what*?'

'Crap. Don't make me say it again, Rio – Matt keeps staring at me every time I say it . . .' We're sitting just one row from the back of the bus, and Syd, Matt and their friends are just behind us.

'So she told your uncle that he's crap at cricket, and then she told your aunt where to get off?'

'Yes. Then they went home.'

'Cool! Sounds like that bump on the head did your mum more good than harm! Sorry — only joking! I wonder what she'd say to *me*! How was she this morning?'

'Seemed OK. Uncle Nigel's going to drop in, to make sure, and to help her in the shop.'

'Right. I like your hair, by the way — *and* your make-up! How did you get past your mum? Doesn't she mind make-up any more?'

'Er . . . I'm not sure.' (If Mum is cool enough to say 'crap', perhaps she'll let me wear make-up!)

'It's really cool the way you've tied your hair back and left the two long bits at the front,' Rio continues.

'Thanks!'

'Do you want to come back to my place after school today? Jaz is going to the doctor, so we're not practising after school.

MY NEW COOL
HAIRSTYLE

Perhaps you can help me go through the song? You're so good at singing — you can listen and tell me what you think! It's about time we got together — I've got things to tell you and *someone* to tell you about . . .' (I'm glad she can fit me into her busy schedule! I wonder if I should be cool and say that I'm busy? But I am overcome by curiosity about the things and the someone. Rio answers all my questions with 'Wait until later!' — *so* annoying!)

Later at the dress (undress?!) rehearsal

The Sistaz of Shame appear on stage in very short shorts, shocking-pink bikini tops and Doc Marten boots. Rio has spiked her hair and is wearing heavy black eyeliner and loud red lipstick.

I clap and cheer with everyone else when they reach the end of their performance, and there are some whoops and wolf-whistles as well.

Suddenly I become aware that someone is peering closely at my face. It is Mr Crotchett.

'Maddy?'

'Yes, sir?'

'Are you wearing make-up?'

'Yes, sir.'

'Go and wash it off, please.'

(Unfair . . . unfair . . . unfair . . . unfair . . .)

Back at Rio's place, in her room

Rio rummages in her underwear drawer (which always looks as though it has just exploded, so that bras, knickers etc are strewn all over the floor). 'Look at these!' she exclaims triumphantly, clutching a handful of assorted thongs. 'They're new. Aren't they cool? Mum got them for me. But I can't decide which to wear for the concert. So I want you to help me choose.'

THONGS

I open and close my mouth several times,

like a fish. 'Your . . . your *mum* got them for you . . .?'

'Yeah. So?'

I am flabbergasted (seldom has my flabber been quite so gasted . . .). Mum would *never* buy me anything like that! Mum is into 'sensible' underwear – at least as far as *I* am concerned. She refers to my undies as 'smalls', which is misleading, as they are quite large. The most recent pack of knickers which she bought for me were in pastel shades of pink, blue, yellow and green, with a motif of cute ballet-dancing hippos. (I'm wearing the pink ones today . . .)

'Maddy, you're either about to throw up or you've never seen a thong before – which is it?'

'Of course I've seen thongs before, but . . . but . . . I don't . . .'

'Have any?'

I nod.

'Would you like some?'

I nod again.

'Well, go on. You can have a couple of these. I can spare them. It's OK – they're brand new. Leave those purple ones with the silver bits – I like those. And let's get changed out of our school stuff. You can borrow some of my clothes – isn't it lucky we're the same size?'

'It really is!' I exclaim. I choose a Union Jack one (to wear now) and one that says 'Love is a many-splendoured thong' in dark blue letters on a pale blue background.

'Thanks, Rio! They're so COOL! Oh, thank you! Now, tell me. Who *is* this mysterious someone you mentioned earlier? Come on – OUT WITH IT!'

'Jack!' says Rio, a dreamy look floating across her face. 'His name's Jack! He is SCRUMMY!'

'So you fancy him?'

'Just a little bit.'

'Does he go to St Swithin's? I can't think of anyone called

JACK

Jack . . . Rio! You don't mean that spotty ginger-haired boy in year eight with the Harry Potter glasses?! Rio! That is serious baby-snatching!' (Rio and I are in year nine.)

'For goodness' sake, Maddy – I do have *some* taste, you know! I'm talking about a different Jack. He was at another school, and he left last year. He's doing gardening and general maintenance work at Mum and Dad's de-stressing place. Dad brought him home late yesterday evening after he'd done some overtime at work over the weekend – he's trying to earn money to go around the world. I want him to take me with him! But he's probably going to take Syd – they got on really well. Oh, and he's brilliant at beatboxing. He is so COOL!'

After nearly forty minutes of listening to Rio going into raptures about Jack, punctuated by several renditions by Rio of her 'song' (I don't know if it's off-key or whether it's *meant* to be like that . . .), I decide that I have heard enough. (I want to go into similar raptures about Syd, but it's embarrassing, because he is Rio's brother. I wonder where he is today – he doesn't seem to be at home.)

'Syd and Jack have gone boarding together,' says Rio, apparently reading my mind, making me jump and blush violently (I feel stupid – why

JACK IS BRILLIANT AT BEATBOXING

shouldn't I fancy her brother? As she said, everyone does . . .)

'Where?' I quaver.

'Oh, just along the wide bit of pavement near the village green – where that parking area is, with the low walls and ramp for wheelchairs. Syd and Jack discovered they're both into boarding, so Syd told Jack to bring his deck along. I expect that's where they've gone.'

Rio and I exchange what-are-we-waiting-for? looks.

'Let's go!' exclaims Rio.

Five minutes later (after hastily doing our hair and re-applying make-up), we're heading for the village green. (I have stuffed my uniform and the many-splendoured thong into my schoolbag, which I've brought with me.) Sure enough, the boys are there, practising stunts on their skateboards. Syd narrowly misses running over a duck, and Jack has to swerve out of the path of old Mr Ricketts, who is hobbling past with Samson the dog – Samson barks excitedly and tries to chase after Jack, nearly pulling Mr Ricketts over.

Jack swerves close to us and grins. I understand why Rio fancies him. He has a ring through his eyebrow, like Syd, *and* one through his lip. (Syd has to put a plaster over his piercing for school.) Jack has a warm and friendly smile – and his trousers are very cool! (But I still prefer Syd . . . *and* his trousers!)

'Uh-oh!' mutters Rio. 'Your mum doesn't look too pleased!'

'Mum? Where?' I look around and see Mum marching towards us from the direction of the Village Stores.

'I think she's on the warpath,' Rio whispers. 'She's not going to have a go at me, is she? Like she did with your aunt?'

MUM ON THE WARPATH !
(SCARY !)

(Mum? On the warpath? This *is* scary – Mum usually keeps to the peacepath.)

But now that she is close enough for me to see the

67

expression on her face, I realise that Rio is right – Mum is seriously unamused . . .

'IDIOT BOYS!!!' she thunders.

Syd and Jack look at each other questioningly. Jack shrugs his shoulders. Samson is still barking, and Mr Ricketts has paused nearby, apparently fascinated.

'*Don't* shrug your shoulders at me, ill-mannered youth!' Mum yells, all red in the face. (I have never seen Mum go red in the face before – this is seriously strange and embarrassing.)

'Are you *completely* stupid?' Mum screeches. 'Only louts like you would even *think* of skateboarding in a disabled parking area – don't you realise how dangerous it is? You nearly *killed* that duck – I saw you! I'm calling the POLICE!!!' she bellows.

'Er . . . er . . . steady on, dear Mrs Mitchell!' Mr Ricketts intervenes. 'Perhaps the boys just didn't think – perhaps they're sorry?' (Mr Ricketts fixes Syd and Jack with a meaningful stare, and they both start nodding . . .) 'Boys will be boys, after all,' he adds.

'You mean idiots will be idiots!' Mum retorts. 'Look at them – with their nasty facial piercings and unpleasant trousers!'

'Muuumm!' I bleat desperately. Mum turns to look at me. 'And as for *you*, Maddy,' (OK, I wish I'd kept my mouth shut . . .) 'you are to go and wash that MUCK *off* your face IMMEDIATELY!'

(By 'muck' I suppose that Mum is referring to my make-up – she may have become more open in expressing her feelings, but she has definitely not become more open-minded . . .)

68

'And where's your school uniform? Why are you wearing that disgusting top?' (It is a black strappy top which says 'Sexy Babe' in pink letters.)

'Rio lent it to me – and it's not disgusting. I've got my uniform in my bag.'

'Show me.'

'Wha . . . what?'

'I said show me your uniform. For all I know, these . . . people . . .' she indicates Rio, Syd and Jack, 'have been encouraging you to skip school.'

'They *haven't*!' I shout back. 'And showing you my uniform won't prove anything!' (I can't remember arguing with Mum like this before – and especially not in front of a gaping audience, which happens to include the boy I most want to appear cool in front of – some chance *now* . . .)

'JUST DO AS YOU'RE TOLD!' Mum shrieks.

(OK – now I'm scared . . .) I unzip my school bag with trembling hands . . . unfortunately the many-splendoured thong comes tumbling out on to the pavement in front of *everyone*. My life is *over* . . .)

'*What* is *that*?!' screams Mum.

'A thong,' I mutter, quickly scooping it up and stuffing it deep into my bag. I pull out my school uniform in an attempt to appease Mum. But Mum seizes the entire bag from me.

'I *hardly* consider THONGS to be appropriate underwear for a girl of your age!' she shouts. (Appropriate for *what*?!) 'I'm confiscating them!'

'You CAN'T DO THAT!!!'

'Oh, I can! And I can see that you're already wearing one. Why don't you pull your trousers up?! I don't understand, Maddy – what's wrong with the sensible knickers I bought you recently – the ones with the ballet-dancing hippos on them . . .?'

OK. I have heard enough. So has everyone else. I turn and run all the way back to my room, tears streaming down my bright red face.

Mum returns shortly afterwards and makes me hand over my Union Jack thong – she already has the other one. (Talk about adding insult to injury!) She tells me that she has a splitting headache – she has suffered persistent headaches since the accident, but stubbornly refuses to 'bother' the doctor – and says that my 'behaviour' is not helping. (What about *her* behaviour?! I find it hard to be sympathetic because she is being so HORRIBLE!)

I lie awake for most of the night – I am deeply, deeply traumatised. The many-splendoured thong incident will haunt me for ever – and now Syd knows that I wear *sensible knickers*. How can I ever face him – or Jack – again? I am Sensible Knickers Girl. I also feel frightened – I want Mum back the way she was. At first I thought it was great when she had a go at Aunty Ann, and said rude words and was open about how she felt – wasn't that exactly what I wanted? But now I wish she'd go back to being nice and polite, and keeping her feelings to herself. The old Mum would be too embarrassed to even mention a word like 'thong' in public! I can't believe I *wanted* her to lose her inhibitions – now I just want her to find them again!

Wednesday – the day of the concert!

'Why weren't you at school yesterday?' Rio asks me as we board the bus to travel to school.

'I was ill. I didn't sleep after . . . you know. And I couldn't face anyone. Even Mum said I looked ill – she said she was sorry if she upset me, and that she loved me, and all that. But she won't give the thongs back.'

'Oh, well – they're only thongs. Don't worry – Syd and Jack are cool. Your mum upset Mr Ricketts, by the way. She insulted his dog – she called Samson a noisy, scruffy cur, which was quite funny . . . only not really.' (Rio has noticed the expression on my face, which registers 'not amused'.)

'Well – forget thongs!' says Rio, attempting to be upbeat and light-hearted. 'We've got songs to think about! It's the concert this evening, Maddy!'

'I know . . .'

The thought of the rapidly approaching concert (just half an hour to go now) is *not* making me feel better . . . I have serious butterflies in my stomach – probably some moths as well. Someone could make a wildlife documentary in there! I don't normally get *this* nervous before a concert – but I've just seen Rio's parents, Syd and Jack take their seats in the audience. To make matters worse, Syd has a video camera!

71

(Is he going to record the exact moment when I get up and sing about a fishy in a dishy, and all my hopes of ever becoming a cool person, rather than Sensible Knickers Girl, are finally extinguished?!) I have been trying to keep my distance from Hannah, Rachel and Daisy, who are looking decidedly *un*cool in their nautical theme outfits, but they keep following me around. If I can at least stand near the Cool Crowd, perhaps Syd will realise that I am cool too, despite my clothes . . .

I am wearing the only stripy top I could find – a long-sleeved top which I had when I was ten. It is far too small, and tight under the arms. I don't possess any three-quarter-length trousers, so I am wearing a pair of trousers which shrank in the wash (that look like trousers which shrank in the wash). I am also wearing a pair of long red and white stripy socks and a red and white spotted headscarf, which is only concealing my new hair style. And *no* make-up.)

COOL – OR WHAT? (NOT).

The hall is filling up . . . there's Mum! (I feel glad that she's there – and worried at the same time, in case she *says* things) She waves, in an embarrassing, overexcited mother sort of way – I give a little wave back. Uncle Nigel is there, too. (Aunty Ann and Mum are not speaking, so Aunty Ann has stayed away – this at least is a relief . . .)

Suddenly Rio comes pushing and jostling her way through the assembling choir and members of the orchestra until she reaches me, panting and obviously distraught.

'Rio! What on earth's wrong?'

'Jaz is ill! She felt really sick and faint, and had to go
just now. And Mr Crotchett is being really sad and saying
we can't do our performance unless I can find someone else
to sing with me! He doesn't think my voice is strong enough
on its own, and Kate doesn't sing – she only plays guitar.
Maddy . . .?'

'You don't mean . . .?'

'Pleeeease! You're my only hope! Mr Crotchett said I could
still do it if you agree to sing – because he likes you! Jaz has
left her clothes for the performance, and you're about the
same size. Oh, pleeease! Pretty please with dollops of cream
on and a *gigantic* cherry!!!'

(It occurs to me that this would be my chance to show the
whole school – and Syd – that I *am* a cool person . . .)

'OK – I'll do it!' (I've already been helping Rio to go
through her song on the bus *and* at home, so I feel I know it
backwards – in fact, it sounds better backwards!)

Rio screams and hugs me. 'Just come round to the back of
the stage after you've done your fishy thing and I'll help you
get ready – we won't have much time, but we'll manage it,
won't we? I love you, Maddy!'

Knowing that this is *not* the end of everything and I have
been given another chance to show the audience (and Syd)
that I am more than just an angelic face and voice – that
there is another side to me! – I no longer mind the fish song
quite so much, and I decide to give it some 'oomph'

(Mr Crotchett will be pleased). So I sing out loud and clear:

> *'Dance to your daddy,*
> *My little laddie.*
> *Dance to your daddy,*
> *My little man.'*

(I suppose it was pretty insensitive of them to make me sing a song about daddies.) And finally (thank God!):

HADDOCK!

> *'Who shall have the haddock*
> *When the bo-at comes in?'*

(For some reason I feel particularly uncool when I have to sing the word 'haddock' – I'm sure you wouldn't catch MC Fatarse rapping about haddocks . . .)

There is a burst of rapturous applause. I can hear Uncle Nigel shouting 'Bravo, Maddy!' Because of the lighting on stage, I can't see if Syd has got his video camera trained on me . . . but I don't want to see because I expect that he and Jack are both laughing at me. I don't care! They ain't seen – or heard – nothin' yet . . . (I feel a momentary sinking sensation as I wonder what Mum's reaction is going to be – but I can't afford to start worrying now . . .)

* * *

Glancing quickly in a mirror backstage, I give a little squeak of surprise. I don't recognise myself! (Perhaps Mum won't recognise me – some hope!) Rio has spiked my hair and drawn around my eyes in thick black eyeliner. It feels weird wearing a bikini top when I am nowhere near a swimming pool, and the shorts are so mini that my knickers are visible over the top of them (front *and* back).

'Rio, you can see my knickers! And they're *sensible* – and GREEN!' I moan despairingly. 'Oh, *why* wouldn't Mum give me those thongs back?!'

'So? Da Sistaz of Shame don't care 'bout nuffin', yeah?' says Rio.

'Er . . . right.'

Rio gives me a hug. 'We're on next,' she says. 'Come on, Maddy – you'll show them!'

(Show them my knickers?)

Once I am on stage I get caught up in the whole thing and stop worrying about the fact that my knickers are showing. I yell 'Em-em-em-em-em-em-music-sick-sick-sick-sick-sick-sick!' into my microphone until my voice starts to go hoarse. Rio leaps around the stage pulling faces, contorting her features and twisting her body into strange attitudes. Unless she has gone mad, this must be part of the act – so I do the same. When the performance is over, there is a profound silence (all the more profound in contrast to the noise of a few seconds ago). One or two people cough. Then Syd calls out, 'Go, Rio!' and starts clapping wildly. Jack joins in, and Rio's parents lead

LET'S ROCK!

I DON'T RECOGNISE MYSELF...

a ripple of applause. (I don't think we're going to be asked to do an encore . . .)

I feel exhilarated and faintly embarrassed at the same time (I'm used to more applause than this!). Time to get changed. As I go offstage, I catch sight of Mum and Uncle Nigel. They both have the same stricken expression on their faces, as if they have just opened the cupboard where the best biscuits are kept and found something horrible and possibly dangerous in there instead . . . Mum is *not* clapping . . .

At the end of the concert Mr Cartridge-Penn stands up to give the vote of thanks.

'We have heard and enjoyed many different musical performances this evening – I myself particularly enjoyed the sea shanties, having pirate blood in my veins passed down to me from Black Jack "Rum-Guzzler" Cartridge-Penn, the

Terror of the High Seas . . . (Some of the parents are looking worried.) But I must also make special mention of a performance which was particularly . . . different, by the Sisters of . . . what was it?

Shame, headmaster.

Thank you, Mr Wheatengreen. Shame! That was it! What sort of music would you call that, Mr Crotchett?

Awful, headmaster!

There is much laughter. Well — really! Rio folds her arms and looks disgusted. She glares at Mr Crotchett.

It was a disgusting performance! shouts a female voice from the audience (Oh, *no* — MUM!!!). It shouldn t be allowed! I hope that the teacher responsible for allowing this fiasco will be sacked!

MR CARTRIDGE-PENN

There is a profound and stunned silence in the hall. I want to DIE! Rio is looking at me accusingly, as if I should be able to do something about my own mother — but I can t! I feel so helpless — and angry and embarrassed.

Mr Cartridge-Penn looks dazed. Er . . . um . . . well, I d like to thank you all for coming to our . . . er . . . splendid concert tonight. I sincerely apologise if any of you have been at all . . . er . . . offended. That was not our intention. Good night. (This is an unusually short speech by Mr Cartridge-Penn, who normally waffles on for hours.)

I notice as we leave the hall that people are giving Mum a wide berth. Rio's parents are looking at her oddly. I have my head down and am avoiding catching anyone's eye.

Suddenly someone claps me on the back. 'Great performance, Maddy!' Syd says, smiling.

'Oh . . . oh . . . thanks!' I feel myself blushing tomato red (but perhaps my life isn't over after all!).

There is an awkward silence as we get into the car to go home – Uncle Nigel is driving. I have washed off as much of the make-up as I can, and changed back into my sailor clothes. Suddenly Mum turns to me, her eyes blazing: 'That was disgraceful, Maddy! You've got a lovely voice, and you're a lovely girl, but you really let yourself – and me – down. The sea shanties were wonderful, especially your solo. But I can't approve of what you did with that Rio girl. That awful song has made my head hurt even more than it does usually – you know I've been getting these really bad headaches ever since the accident. You are *not* to associate with Rio any more, do you understand?'

'But . . . but it was only a bit of fun! It's not *fair*!'

(Mum can't *stop* me seeing Rio. She's my friend. And it's MY life . . .)

Chapter Seven

Beware!
Mum on the Loose!

ON THE BUS, going home.

It has been a weird day at school after last night's concert. Hannah, Rachel and Daisy have been giving me strange looks and sort of backing away whenever I've gone anywhere near them – I'm not sure what their problem is. I can't help feeling hurt, even though I'd rather be part of the Cool Crowd, and I'm still getting a nice, tingly sensation whenever I think about Syd clapping me on the back. (OK – so getting clapped on the back isn't quite snogging, but it's a start!) I am feeling a weird mixture of complex emotions at the moment: anxiety about Mum and other people's reactions to her – I feel protective towards her, and half-angry and half-scared at the same time – and bubbling around in this seething cauldron of emotions are my feelings towards Syd!

Rio looks closely at me. 'You look pretty ill,' she observes. 'Bus-sickness?'

'I *was* feeling fine until you said that! Thanks!' I give her a friendly push (at least she's still talking to me). 'But I didn't get much sleep last night – I was worried about Mum. She was so embarrassing at the concert – and I also got thinking what if anything happened . . . to . . . to her? There's only her and me. And what if she makes everyone hate us?'

'But that's *not* going to happen!' says Rio. 'You've got me! How can you possibly be sad when you've got *me* as a friend?!'

(I can't help smiling. Rio's mad – and I'm glad that she's my friend . . .)

Rio tells me that *she* didn't sleep much last night either. She was too hyped up after the concert, and she couldn't stop thinking about Jack . . . She lowers her voice, and explains that she doesn't want Syd to hear what she's saying because he keeps teasing her about having a crush on his friend. 'But he's coming over later!' she whispers excitedly. 'I heard Syd talking to him on his mobile. I can't *wait*! Try to come round to my place – you'd like to, wouldn't you? You'll have to go home and get changed first – I don't want Jack seeing us in our sad school uniform!'

'Mum won't let me come to see you. I know I said she couldn't stop me, and I'd come anyway, but I don't want to risk making her cross. She's been seriously scary recently. You may have noticed.'

'Oh, pleeeease! Talk about a mega-wimp! She can't be *that* bad! Just come straight home with me, if you like, and I'll lend you some more of my clothes . . .'

I haven't told anyone at school about Mum's accident, not even when Mr Wheatengreen congratulated me on singing the fishy song so beautifully and asked after Mum (he seemed genuinely concerned about her). What was I supposed to say? That she got hit on the head by a cricket ball and started saying rude words? I think not. I'm quite relieved that Rio has persuaded me to go home with her – I can forget, for a while, that I have a mad mother . . .

Back at her house, Rio lends me a pair of baggy jeans with loads of pockets and flappy bits, and a skate belt (which is just as well, as the trousers are too big and fall down without the belt).

'Let them slip down a *bit*,' Rio advises. 'It looks better. Oh, you're wearing yellow knickers . . . BIG yellow knickers . . . On second thoughts, you'd better pull the trousers *up* a bit. I'd give you another one of my thongs, but I won't have any left!'

'That's OK.'

'Now you need a top – how about this one? Thanks for returning the other one, by the way – at least your mum didn't confiscate it!'

SENSIBLE KNICKERS

'She was going to – if I didn't get it back to you double quick!'

Rio hands me another black strappy top, this time with a picture of a puckered-up, red-lipsticked mouth on it, and underneath are two words printed in red: 'Kiss me!'

'And you never know,' says Rio, 'someone might get the message! You can borrow some more make-up if you like – try this eyeshadow . . .'

I'm in a happy mood and feeling a lot better than I did this morning. When we'd got to Marsh Cottage, Rio's dad had welcomed me in as though I was part of the family (her mum is working at the de-stressing place and should be back soon, bringing Jack with her). They are such a friendly family – I *wish* Mum would realise how nice they were . . . (But I feel less happy when I think of how difficult it has become to talk to Mum – her opinions are so strong, and her voice seems to have got louder, and she shouts me down if I disagree with her . . .)

'Quick! Maddy – they're here!' squeals Rio excitedly, after a brief glance out of her bedroom window, which is at the front of the house. 'Syd and Jack! OK, OK – I've got to calm down! Take deep breaths! I don't want to be too obvious. I know! We'll go down to the kitchen and get a drink. Syd always takes his friends into the kitchen when they arrive – they all raid the cupboards and fridge. It drives Mum mad!'

'Don't talk about mad mothers!'

'Sorry, but you've got to help me, Maddy! We've got to think of reasons to go wherever the boys are. I want to be in the same room as Jack *all* the time!'

'What if he goes to the loo?'

'Don't be stupid, Maddy! Come on!'

Rio goes to the fridge and gets out a two-litre bottle of Coke. 'Either of you boys want a drink?' she says casually to Syd and Jack, who are standing nearby eating bags of crisps.

'No, I'm OK,' says Jack.

'I'll have that bottle when you've finished with it,' says Syd.

Rio's mum is chopping an onion. 'How's your mum, Maddy?' she asks, her eyes going red and watering. 'Sorry, it's the onion! Rio told me that she'd been hit on the head by a cricket ball and had to go to hospital. And we were a bit worried about her at the concert. It must be difficult for you.'

I feel myself blushing. Rio's mum seems to understand how I am feeling without the need for me to say anything. (I no longer want Mum to express *her* feelings – I want her to understand *mine*! I want her to *listen*!)

Syd and Jack have finished their crisps, and Syd is glugging from the two-litre Coke bottle. I can't help ogling him, and wondering if he's going to drink the lot.

'For goodness' sake, Syd!' exclaims Mrs de Havilland impatiently. 'Use a glass!'

'Sorry, Mum!' says Syd, wiping his mouth on his sleeve.

'And stop wiping your mouth on your sleeve!'

'Sorry!'

(So Mum was wrong when she said that there was no parental control or direction at Rio's house – there seems to be plenty!)

'Jack and I are going to walk down to the village green, Mum. We might go paddling in the Wee. There's nothing else to do round here! We're not allowed to use our decks.'

(I avoid catching Syd's eye – it was Mum who stopped the boys from skateboarding.)

'OK, dear,' says his mum.

Rio gives me a look, as if to say: 'Think of something – *quick*!' Then her face lights up. 'Do you need anything from the shop, Mum? Maddy and I could get it for you.'

I stare at Rio, my eyes wide with alarm, my mouth framing the word 'noooooo!'

'That's very kind of you, darling. I could do with another bottle of Coke, two pints of semi-skimmed, and a tin of tomatoes for the spag bol. Here's some money . . .'

'Are you completely *mad*?' I ask Rio as we head off along the road that slopes gently uphill all the way to Little Bunbury (the River Wee trickles gently down one side of the road, just beyond a small bank of grass and leafy bushes and trees). The boys are a short distance ahead of us and have so far not looked back – I don't know if they are aware that we are behind them.

'It's OK,' says Rio. 'I'll go on my own and do the shopping – your mum can't exactly ban me from the shop, can she? She won't know that we're together. You can stay outside and keep watch on the boys. Right?'

'I suppose so . . .'

Syd and Jack have kicked off their trainers, rolled up their trousers, and are kicking water at each other in the Wee, shouting and laughing. Jack pulls off his T-shirt, so that he is bare-chested. Rio is transfixed. 'Wow!' she breathes.

'Er – isn't it a bit obvious, standing here and staring?' I ask. 'I think they've seen us.' (They couldn't really fail to – we're just a stone's throw away.)

'I . . . don't . . . care!' says Rio, in a faraway voice.

Jack rolls his T-shirt into a ball and throws it at Rio.

'Catch!' he shouts. Rio catches it, and hugs it to her.

'It smells of HIM!' she says ecstatically.

Rio says that she has jelly legs, so we sit down on the grass for a while, watching the boys splashing about and kicking water at each other.

The sun is still shining, but I notice that dark clouds are rolling up across the sky. Finally they move across the sun, and Rio shivers. 'I wish I'd brought my hoody,' she says. Big, fat raindrops begin to fall, and the rain comes down like someone has turned on a shower, full blast, all over our heads.

RIO HAS JELLY LEGS...

'Quick! Into the Village Stores until this stops!' shouts Syd. He and Jack race across the village green in their bare feet and disappear into the shop.

'We *can't*!' I yell at Rio.

'Why NOT?' she shouts. 'Your mum can't rule bar us from the shop – she wouldn't want us to die of pneumonia, would she? Besides, I want to be wherever Jack is! You can stay in the rain if you like!' And she runs off after the boys.

Oh, this is stupid! Rio's right – Mum wouldn't want me to stay outside in a downpour. I race after the others, my trousers soaking up water and slopping uncomfortably around my ankles.

Bursting through the door of the Village Stores, breathless and dripping, I am greeted by the sight of Syd and Jack, wet from head to toe, standing in two little muddy puddles of rainwater, which is still dripping off them. There are muddy footprints (size eleven-ish) leading from the door and over to where they are standing, and they seem to have brought a fair amount of village green into the shop with them, stuck to the soles of their feet. Rio is standing just slightly apart from them, also dripping, her trousers soaked almost to the knee.

It is very quiet. I am aware of the sound of the rain thrumming on the ground outside. There are other people in the shop, but no one is talking, or moving. Blinking the rain-drops out of my eyes (I feel sure that the mascara which Rio lent me must have smudged and run down my cheeks, and my hair is sticking to my face – I hope Syd goes for the drowned panda look!!!), I look around the shop and see that Mum, Aunty Ann, Uncle Nigel, Mr Battlefield and Mrs Partridge are all staring hard at Syd, Jack and Rio – and at me! Mum and Aunty Ann are staring particularly hard at Jack. (Have Mum and Aunty Ann made it up?)

Uncle Nigel is the first to make a sound, or move. He starts humming a little tune, and carries on with his shopping, filling

his basket with onions, curry powder, mango chutney and other ingredients.

'Disgraceful!' barks Aunty Ann suddenly, making everyone jump. 'I warned you about the sort of young people Maddy was getting mixed up with, Helen! I told you no good would come of it! Look at the mess they've made of your nice, clean floor! Mud everywhere! And look at Maddy – she never used to look like that until she met *them*!' She jabs a plump finger in the direction of Syd, Jack and Rio.

'I can't help looking like this, Aunty Ann – it was *raining*!'

'SILENCE!' bellows Aunty Ann. 'You *never* used to answer back before, young lady! Now you do it all the time! And where did you get that vulgar and tasteless top you're wearing?'

'Be quiet, Ann!' shouts Mum. 'I can deal with my own daughter, thank you very much – so stay out of it, you interfering and thoroughly bossy old bat!'

(Mum's Foot-in-Mouth disease is getting worse . . . Despite my delight at hearing Mum tell Aunty Ann to leave me alone, I'm feeling a little sorry for my trembling aunt. I have a weird, half-funny, half-disturbing, mental image of mum attacking a jelly with an enormous metal spoon – SPLAT! I am also worried about how exactly Mum is intending to 'deal' with me . . .)

'Well – REALLY!' splutters Aunty Ann, wobbling badly. (If Mum and Aunty Ann *did* make it up, I think they have just fallen out again – *big* time!) 'Come on, Nigel – let's go!'

'But I haven't finished my shopping, dear!'

'Your sister has just insulted me – again! You heard her!'

'I don't think Helen is quite herself yet, dear. I'm sure she didn't mean to offend you . . .'

'Yes, I *did*!' exclaims Mum triumphantly.

'Helen, *please*, be quiet,' says Uncle Nigel in a low voice. Then, to his wife: 'You go home, if you like, dear – you'd better fetch Foofy from upstairs. But I'm going to stay and cook supper for Helen and Maddy. After all, it was my fault that the . . . the accident happened . . . I think I *should* cook them supper! I'll be back later!'

Aunty Ann sniffs loudly. 'It's a sad day when a husband doesn't stand up for his wife!' she says. 'Don't expect me to make you any cocoa tonight, Nigel!' And she marches through the door at the back of the shop, on her way to fetch Foofy.

'Oh, dear!' says Uncle Nigel. 'I think I've upset her!'

'Good for you!' exclaims Mum. 'I'm sick to death of my brother behaving like a downtrodden, hen-pecked little worm!'

For a moment I think that Uncle Nigel is going to walk out,

PECK PECK

'I'M SICK OF MY BROTHER BEHAVING LIKE A DOWNTRODDEN, HEN-PECKED LITTLE WORM!'

too. But he makes a mammoth effort and says, rather stiffly, 'If I could just pay for this shopping, Helen, I think I'll go upstairs and start cooking.'

Aunty Ann sweeps past with Foofy in her arms, brushing Uncle Nigel out of the way and making a grand exit.

'I think we'd better go,' mutters Syd. 'I'm soaked.'

'*Not* so fast!' shouts Mum. 'I want a word with you!' (She's right – there is *nothing* wrong with her hearing.)

Mr Battlefield starts chuckling. 'Wait until I tell Doris about this!' he says. 'She won't believe it – I only came in for some lemons!'

'That seems appropriate,' Mum remarks. 'Doris looks as though she spends her days sucking lemons.'

'Mrs Mitchell – I must protest!' exclaims Mr Battlefield. 'You are talking about the woman I love!'

'I'm only stating the truth, Mr Battlefield,' Mum replies.

'Sometimes,' Mr Battlefield remarks, 'the truth is better left unsaid. Good day to you.' And he leaves the shop *without* raising his hat.

'I think you just lost another customer,' observes Jack.

Mum gives him a deeply withering look. 'As for *you*,' she says (uh oh – here we go . . .), '*You* and *him* . . .' she nods towards Syd ' . . . YOU are clearly a BAD INFLUENCE!'

'DORIS LOOKS AS THOUGH SHE SPENDS HER DAYS SUCKING LEMONS ! '

'On who? Why? What?' Jack falters. 'Please – would someone explain what's going on here? I only came in to shelter from the rain!'

'You and your facial piercings!' roars Mum. 'Because of people like *you*, impressionable young girls like Maddy think it's clever to drill holes in their faces!'

'Actually, they don't use a drill . . .' Jack starts to explain.

'... THEY DON'T USE A DRILL ...'

'BE QUIET!!!' shouts Mum. 'I don't like you! And the *reason* I don't like you is because you have a ring through your lip and another one through your right eyebrow. And it wouldn't matter if it was through your left eyebrow – or any other eyebrow. I *still* wouldn't like you!'

'But that's not fair!' Rio bursts out. 'You can't say that you don't like Jack just because he's had his lip and eyebrow pierced! It's not fair to judge someone by their appearance, especially when you don't even know them!'

'I know *enough*,' says Mum. 'And I know that you are a wilful young lady who has *far* too much to say for herself, not all of it very polite!'

'Well, *you're* not very polite!' retorts Rio angrily.

'Until Maddy met *you*,' shouts Mum, 'she *never* answered back, she wore *nice* clothes and SENSIBLE KNICKERS . . .'

(Oh no. Not again.)

'. . . AND,' continues Mum, relentlessly, 'Maddy would *never* have sung such an awful song, if it wasn't for you! She's got a lovely voice, and it was *horrifying* seeing what you did to her! Those clothes! That horrible make-up! *Look* at her! Because of you, she's got make-up all over her face!'

'It was the rain, Mum!' I protest. 'The mascara's run, that's all! Please leave Rio alone – none of what you just said is *her* fault. I'm just being *ME*! Why can't you understand? I am *not* copying Rio – I'm just changing – growing up. Why can't you accept it?' I shout, shaking all over. (I am not used to shouting, especially not at Mum – and I am *not* used to Mum shouting back!)

Rio looks really upset, as though she is about to cry.

'Why don't you leave my sister alone?' says Syd. 'She's not *your* daughter!'

Mum turns to look at Syd. 'I expect it's largely *your* fault,' she says. 'Are you on drugs? I've noticed that you never brush your hair. People on drugs never bother to brush their hair.'

Syd shakes his head (and drops of water fly in all directions). 'I've had enough of this,' he says. 'Let's go.'

They all start to leave, including Rio.

'Rio!' I call out. But she doesn't look back.

'Mum!' I shout angrily. 'How could you? Those are – or *were* – my friends!'

'Don't you *dare* raise your voice to me, young lady!' Mum shouts back. 'You are NOT to go on seeing Rio and that drug-crazed brother of hers, or their strange friend. DO YOU UNDERSTAND?' (Mum roars this last bit! I have *never* heard Mum roar before – I feel all shaky . . .)

I decide to keep quiet. Mum has just emptied her shop of customers (Mrs Partridge slipped out quietly before Mum could have a go at her too). My eyes keep filling with tears at the thought of the humiliation I have just endured. Syd must now think of me as a giggling, tongue-tied idiot who wears sensible knickers and has a mad mother, and Mum has probably lost me my best friend. I also feel frightened – I don't even recognise Mum as the same Mum whom I have known and loved all these years. She has become totally un-Mum-like. She used to have a lovely smile, but now she frowns most of the time and looks cross. I wish I could take a giant eraser, rub out the frown lines and the downturned mouth and pencil in a happy smile. Then I try to think of more practical ways of making Mum smile instead of frowning and shouting. Should I tidy my room? Fill the house with flowers? Tell her I love her? It's difficult when she has probably just lost me my friends. My eyes fill with tears . . .

Soon my eyes are filling with tears for a different reason – Uncle Nigel's curry is *hot*! *Very hot!!!* (How many chilies?!) Uncle Nigel blows his nose, wipes his eyes with a paper napkin and pours himself another glass of water, which he glugs down, and then pours another . . . When he has recovered enough to speak, he turns to Mum and asks, in a concerned voice, 'How *are* you, Helen?'

UNCLE NIGEL'S CURRY IS HOT!

'My headache's nearly gone,' Mum replies. 'But I seem to be suffering from a most awful wind problem – this curry isn't going to help! I've been farting like a trooper all day! In fact, it's even worse than that! I've been farting almost as badly as Foofy!'

(This is definitely *too much information*, and I make a mental note to avoid asking Mum how she is in future . . .)

Another restless night . . .

It is Friday, and Rio is not at school today. At lunch-time I take a deep breath and summon the courage to approach Syd to ask him where Rio is. I nearly turn and run away when I see him look in my direction and then whisper something to Matt (he's probably saying, 'Look out – here comes Sensible Knickers Girl'!). He probably hates me after everything that Mum said yesterday. I don't even know if Rio is still talking to me . . .

'Er . . . hello, Syd!'

'Maddy! How's things?' (He seems friendly!)

'I . . . I'm reeeeally sorry about yesterday!'

'Don't worry about it. I've got parents, too – remember? They can all go a bit weird sometimes. Just forget it.'

(Syd is soooooooooooooo cool! Just like he was at the concert. I shouldn't have worried. I have jelly legs again . . .)

'Th . . . th . . . th . . . thanks!' I lisp, and a little bit of spit shoots out of my mouth. (WHY? Why does it happen to ME?!)

'Wh . . . where's Rio?' I ask, trying desperately to sound casual.

'At home, I think. Not feeling too good.'

'Oh . . .'

'Why don't you come round later – see how she is? I'm sure that would cheer her up!'

I nod. (But I'm not sure. What if she's told her parents what happened? Will they even let me in the house? But I *must* talk to her . . . try to explain . . . I need *someone* to talk to . . .)

Rio's dad opens the door.

'Hello, Maddy! Come in! Rio's bored out of her mind – she'll be so pleased to see you. Have you come straight from school?'

'Yes.' (Rio's dad is so friendly – I wonder if he knows about Mum. Rio doesn't realise how lucky she is to have such a nice dad . . .)

I find Rio in her room.

'What's up?' I ask.

'Nothing. Just a headache.'

(A slight pause.)

'Are you still talking to me?' I ask. 'I mean – after yesterday?'

'Why shouldn't I be?'

'Er . . . because of Mum?'

Rio shrugs and pulls a face. 'Look, Maddy – it's not your fault if your mum hates me. It just means that I can't come round to your place, and it's going to make hanging out together difficult. I didn't realise how bad it was until I was in the shop yesterday.'

(This doesn't sound like Rio. I thought Rio didn't care what other people think. But she seems to care rather a lot . . .)

'Mum doesn't hate you! She's just . . . confused. Like Uncle Nigel says – she's "not herself". It's like she's someone else. She doesn't listen to me any more.' I feel a slight choking and a prickling sensation behind my eyes, but I make an effort at self-control. 'I keep hoping she'll just go back to how she used to be, before she got hit on the head by that cricket ball. She's still my mum, but now she . . . says things. In fact, she shouts them.'

'She certainly does!'

'I wish she'd see a doctor. Uncle Nigel and I keep trying to persuade her, but she won't listen. She thinks she's fine.'

'I still can't hang out with you.'

'STOP SAYING THAT, RIO!' I burst out suddenly, and tears start streaming down my face.

Rio looks taken aback. 'Maddy! Please don't cry!' She puts

her arm around me. 'What's wrong, honey?' she asks gently.

'Everything!' I sob. 'My whole life! You're the only person I can talk to – *please* don't stop hanging out with me! I'm living with a mad mother, and I've got nowhere to go – except here – and . . . and I'm scared!'

'OK . . . OK . . . it's OK!' says Rio soothingly. 'I'm still your friend. I said it would be *difficult* to hang out with you. But I guess it's not impossible . . .'

'Oh, thank you, Rio!' I give her a hug. 'You're a real friend! I can't talk to Hannah, Rachel or Daisy. They've been acting like I'm some kind of freak ever since the concert, and they're probably saying stuff about me behind my back. That's what they do.'

'*They're* the freaks, Maddy – you don't need them. You've got *me* – OK?'

'OK.' We smile at each other.

'Friends?' I say.

'Friends!' says Rio.

'By the way did you tell your parents?' I ask.

'No, I didn't. I didn't want to talk about it – and I still don't. So I came straight up to my room and shut the door. Mum and Dad knew that something was wrong – Dad wanted to hold a family powwow. But I refused. I told them I was ill.'

'But you're better now?'

'Yes. I'm better now.'

I wish Mum was better now. But I know that there is something *seriously* strange still going on with her when I arrive home to

HAVE YOU SEEN MY MUM'S INHIBITIONS? IT'S REALLY IMPORTANT SHE HAS THEM BACK...

LOST PROPERTY

find an ENORMOUS fluffy ginger cat sitting in the living room in Foofy's little velvet-lined basket (which is kept here for him). The cat is so large that his fur is spilling over the edges of the basket. Mum is kneeling down, making cooing noises and spoon-feeding the cat tinned salmon from the little silver dish normally reserved for Foofy.

'Mum? What . . .?' (Words fail me.)

'Oh, hello, Maddy! Meet Augustus.'

'Augustus?'

'Augustus the Cat. Say "How do you do?", Augustus. Say "How do you do?", Maddy.'

'Mum! We can't have a cat! You always said it wouldn't be fair, keeping it cooped up over the shop!'

'Augustus has already found his way down the stairs and out into the garden, haven't you, Augustus? But I want to keep

him indoors as much as possible
to begin with – I don't want him
finding his way back to his old
home. There's a
litter tray in the
kitchen in case
he's caught
short.'

AUGUSTUS

(Great!)

'But, Mum – what about Foofy?'

'What *about* Foofy? I decided that it was high time that
we had a proper pet, rather than that bad-tempered,
overindulged apology for a dog. Like owner, like pet, if you
ask me.'

So it's personal. This is Mum's way of getting at Aunty Ann.
But isn't it going a bit too far . . .?

'Mum – where *did* you get Augustus?'

(I can't help but worry that Mum may have turned into a cat
burglar – literally!)

'I got him from the lady who advertised kittens on our
noticeboard downstairs – Mrs Petheridge. I went round to her
house this morning – I wanted it to be a nice surprise for you
when you got home from school. But all the kittens had gone.
I noticed that she still had lots of cats – there must have been
eight or more of them, milling and mewing around our legs. I
told Mrs Petheridge that it was unhygienic and unsanitary,
having so many cats!'

'Oh . . .'

100

'And then this one . . .' Mum puts down the spoon and strokes Augustus '. . . this one followed me home. So I said he could stay, if he wanted to. It's one less for Mrs Petheridge to have to bother about. OUCH!'

'Did he bite you?'

'Yes. I think it was affection.'

(I think it wasn't. On closer inspection I notice that Augustus has a torn ear and a scar above one eye . . .)

'Mum, I don't think Augustus has been operated on. He might make the place smell. And don't you think Mrs Petheridge might want her cat back?'

Mum looks doubtful. 'She comes to the shop quite often. If she says anything, I'll tell her I've found her cat.'

'*Found* him? You've *catnapped* him!'

'Don't be so over-dramatic, Maddy! He obviously *wanted* a new home.'

'And he smells.'

'Then I shall take him to the vet. But not yet. He needs time to settle in. Don't you, Gus?' She strokes him on the head. Gus emits a low, warning growl. Then he turns round in the basket several times and settles down to sleep, with his back to us.

'I think he's tired,' says Mum. 'Let's leave him. He needs his beauty sleep.'

Chapter Eight

Parents' Evening

RIO WAS AWAY all weekend with her parents, visiting her grandmother. They didn't get back until late on Monday evening, so it is Tuesday when I next see her. I am really glad when I catch up with her, boarding the bus. (Mum has been driving me mad all weekend, cooing over Augustus, and ignoring me when I try to suggest that she should: a) see a doctor, b) return Mrs Petheridge's cat, and c) listen to me!)

But Rio is in a mood. When I tell her about Augustus, she just grunts and says, 'The cat probably won't like me, either.'

'Augustus doesn't like anyone – except Mum, sometimes, when he's not biting her. Why are you in a mood?'

'I'm *not* in a mood. I'm just fed up because it's parents' evening tonight, and Mum and Dad are insisting on going to it. I don't want them to go. They're *so* embarrassing! The concert was bad enough! Did you see Dad stand up and applaud, when hardly anyone else was? And then he started whooping. What kind of parent WHOOPS?!'

'Oh . . . my . . . God!' I exclaim.

'Are you OK, Maddy?' Rio asks. 'You've gone green. Is it bus-sickness?'

'No – I'd forgotten all about parents' evening! I gave Mum the letter and made her appointments and everything before the accident – the letter's on the shelf in the kitchen. Just imagine what it's going to be like . . .' I shudder. 'And you think *your* parents are embarrassing! Although . . .' I pause thoughtfully. 'Maybe Mum could put Mrs Cogg in her place, like she did with Aunty Ann. Mrs Cogg has been giving me a *really* hard time recently – and it's not fair. I do *try* to stay awake in her lessons.'

Mum has not forgotten about parents' evening. I find her in her bedroom with Augustus, searching through her wardrobe for something to wear.

'Parents' evening tonight!' she says, as soon as she sees me. 'I closed the shop early so that I could get ready. Didn't seem to have many customers, for some reason. Strange . . .'

(It is not strange. It is hardly surprising – Mum has managed to offend nearly all her regular customers, which is nearly everyone in the village, in the last couple of days . . .)

'Now – what do you think I should wear? This? Or this?' She holds up a flirty short pink evening dress in one hand and a green suit with flared skirt and bolero jacket in the other. (The skirt looks like a badly made lampshade . . .) I am about to say something along the lines of 'Over my dead body do you appear at school wearing either of those!' when I realise that she is not asking me – she is asking Augustus!

Something snaps inside me. 'Don't you care what *I* think?' I exclaim. 'Don't you care about me at all? You only seem to care about the cat!' (My own complex emotions are getting the better of me . . . jealousy of the cat is just one of my increasingly weird feelings – I need my mum back!)

Mum looks taken aback. She comes over and puts her arms around me. 'Of *course* I care about you, Maddy! I love you!' She looks into my eyes, and I look back. She is still my mum . . .

'I love you too, Mum!' I tell her. And she SMILES! Suddenly she looks just like she used to – my lovely, kind, NORMAL Mum!

Then reality comes crashing down on my head. It is time to go to parents' evening. (There is no way that I can get out of this – I am DOOMED! *Unless* . . . Mum goes on smiling, doesn't say anything strange and dresses normally – some chance!)

She has opted to wear the green suit, with a pair of knee-length black boots. She looks like a member of a dance troupe from a small Eastern European country.

We set off in Mum's beloved blue Mini. She has always been an erratic driver, and I spend most of the journey with my eyes tight shut, my breath held and my knuckles turning white (I can hear ducks quacking and scattering in all directions as we lurch along the High Street, past the village green – we usually travel everywhere on a full tank of kangaroo juice . . .).

My nerves are already in shreds when we arrive at parents' evening. Everyone else's parents look so *normal*. Why do I

THE SKIRT IS LIKE A BADLY-MADE LAMPSHADE

MUM LOOKS LIKE A MEMBER OF A DANCE TROUPE...

have a parent who looks like a member of an Eastern European dance troupe?!

'Where to first?' asks Mum.

'Home,' I say.

'Come on, Maddy! I'm here to see your teachers. Take me to a teacher!'

With a strong sense of impending doom, I look at my list and see that our first appointment is with Mr Poole, the physics teacher. (He is the teacher whom we refer to, jokingly, as Satan behind his back, not because he is mean – he is actually very friendly – but because of his little black goatee and slanty black eyebrows.)

Mum shakes Mr Poole's hand (so far, so good!), and we both sit down at his table.

'Maddy's doing very well . . .' he begins. Then he hesitates, as he has noticed that Mum is staring at him – hard – and frowning.

MR POOLE
(KNOWN AS 'SATAN'. . .)

'Is there something you wanted to ask me, Mrs Mitchell?' he enquires. 'Some worry or concern? I assure you that Maddy is doing very well . . .'

'You look like the devil,' says Mum.

'Pardon?'

'I said you look like the devil.'

'Oh. Er . . . perhaps we could get back to talking about Maddy's work, which has been quite excellent, as usual . . .'

'It must be very distracting for your students, having a teacher who looks like the devil,' Mum continues, warming to her theme.

(Hannah is standing nearby with her parents, and she is listening hard, her mouth gaping. WHY doesn't the floor just open and swallow me up??! Why doesn't that dried-up pot plant in the corner of the room suddenly leap out of its pot and chase everyone home? Something unexpected like that would certainly shift the focus away from me and Mum!)

'Mrs Mitchell!' exclaims Mr Poole. 'Please! I really must protest!'

'If you want your class to concentrate,' says Mum, 'which I assume you do, then you must shave off your beard. It must be very distracting for your class to have a teacher who looks like the devil. Your eyebrows are quite distracting, too – but I think it would be a mistake to shave them off, as you would look even stranger without them. Of course, I understand that you may very well have a weak chin, which is the only excuse for growing a beard. If that is the case, and you feel that you cannot do without a beard, then you should grow a full beard. A full beard wouldn't make you look like the devil. Then your class could concentrate on their work, and they would get better results. Thank you for seeing us, Mr Poole, and I am glad that Maddy is doing so well. Good evening.'

Mum's Foot-in-Mouth disease has now become ACUTE and CHRONIC. I hope it's not hereditary – what if *I* get hit on the head by a cricket ball one day? Will I behave like this – or worse?! I think about all the times I've worried about saying *seriously* inappropriate things aloud by mistake – things that I meant to only *think*! And now that Mum has actually *said* some of these things to Mr Poole, How can I EVER face him – or his goatee – again? I am amazed that Mum had the same thoughts as I did about Mr Poole's resemblance to Satan and I realise, with a strange pang of recognition and affection, that we must be more alike than I had thought – what's that old expression about 'great minds think alike'? But I am also beyond humiliated by the fact that Mum actually expressed these thoughts to Mr Poole, which I would *never* do. The pendulum on my Embarrassometer has swung to EXTREME.

Leaving Mr Poole looking dazed, Mum gets up and peers at my list of appointments. 'Who's next?' she asks, with a slightly manic gleam in her eye.

'Mum – please can we go home? I don't feel well.'

'Nonsense, Maddy! You look fine. We're here now, and we might as well see some more of your teachers. So – who's next?'

'Mr Wheatengreen. Geography.'

Mr Wheatengreen beams with pleasure as he sees Mum approaching his table. He gets up and shakes her warmly by the hand. 'Mrs Mitchell! How lovely to see you! How are you?'

(Uh-oh. WRONG question . . .)

'Well,' says Mum, seating herself opposite Mr Wheatengreen, 'the bump on my head is a lot smaller now, and I would recommend frozen peas to anyone – especially for headaches! I got through six family-size bags in two days!' (Of course Mr Wheatengreen hasn't a clue about Mum's accident – he probably thinks that she ate the peas rather than wearing them on her head!)

'Unfortunately my wind problem has got worse,' Mum continues. 'I must have sounded like a car backfiring all last night!' she says with a laugh. 'Hope I didn't disturb you, Maddy!'

I give a ghastly grin. I can't breathe. There seems to be no air in the room.

The smile on Mr Wheatengreen's face freezes, then slowly fades. 'Perhaps if you ate a few less peas?' he suggests tentatively.

'PERHAPS IF YOU ATE A FEW LESS PEAS...?'

ME – DYING OF EMBARRASSMENT

← MR WHEATENGREEN

'What do you mean?' says Mum sharply. 'I don't like peas!'

Mr Wheatengreen looks confused.

'Would you like to know how Maddy's getting on in geography?' asks Mr Wheatengreen.

'Splendidly?' Mum asks in a bored tone of voice.

'Yes – how did you know?' says Mr Wheatengreen, looking uncomfortable.

'Because that's what you always say,' says Mum. 'I find your comments uninformative and unoriginal.'

Leaving Mr Wheatengreen mouthing helplessly at Mum like a stranded fish, I escape to talk to Rio, whom I have spotted walking past in the corridor with her parents, making their way to another of the rooms where parents' evening is taking place.

'Rio!'

'Maddy!'

We hug each other. 'It's as if they haven't seen each other for years!' says Rio's dad with a laugh. Her mum smiles. (There is nothing embarrassing about Rio's parents, if you ignore the fact that her dad is wearing a straw hat, set at a jaunty angle and decorated with a rainbow-coloured ribbon. At least her mum isn't carrying the pipe of peace with her!)

'Is your mum here, Maddy?' Rio's mum asks.

As if in answer to this question, there is a cry of 'Maddy! *There* you are!' and Mum comes hurrying towards us down the corridor. 'I lost you!' she says breathlessly. (She looks so pleased to see me! I *want* to feel close to her, but she keeps saying things to people which make me want to run away and hide!)

As soon as Mum catches sight of Rio she looks cross again.

'And I don't think you should be talking to *this* young lady, do you?' she says, indicating Rio with a slight motion of her head.

Rio's parents look surprised.

'Mum!' I say. 'These are Rio's parents, Mr and Mrs de Havilland.' I give Mum a beseeching look – *pleeeeease* be nice!

'We saw you at the concert,' says Rio's mum, making an

effort to be friendly, despite Mum's comment. 'Our girls certainly put on a spirited performance, didn't they?'

'Spirited? Is that what you'd call it? I thought it was DISGRACEFUL! But I suppose that you alternative types like to encourage your children to behave in a loud and offensive manner – you want them to "express themselves". As far as *I* am concerned, you have brought up your children in *entirely* the wrong way, allowing them *far* too much freedom to do as they please, without respect for the feelings or the property of others. And – let's face it – without proper respect for themselves, which is why they wear too much make-up, do ridiculous things with their hair and drill holes in their own faces! And I *really* object when my own daughter comes under the influence of the bad behaviour which YOU have encouraged! And I do NOT like the sound of that pipe of peace!!! Whatever happened to proper parental control and responsibility?'

Rio's parents look stunned. Rio looks shocked and angry. 'My parents are the BEST!' she shouts. 'Leave them alone!' (I have gone cold inside – my heart has turned to stone and is sinking slowly down to the pit of my stomach.)

'Huh! Answering back as USUAL!' says Mum to Rio with an I-told-you-so glance at Rio's parents.

I can see that Rio's dad is having a really hard internal struggle between his philosophy of tolerance and understanding other people's points of view, and his reaction as a normal person. In the end, normal person wins the day!

'How DARE you!' he explodes. 'Rio is an extremely well-brought-up girl, and neither she, nor her mother or I, deserve

111

to be insulted! Our children have been brought up to have considerably more respect for the feelings of others than *you* appear to have!'

'Come on, dear!' says Rio's mum, taking her husband's arm and pulling him away. 'We need to go and see Mr Edmondson – we mustn't be late for our appointment.' She walks away without another word, not even looking at Mum. I can tell that she is very upset from the expression on her face – she is almost in tears.

Rio and I exchange despairing looks, but there is nothing we can do. Rio has to go with her parents, and I trail sadly after Mum, enduring the stares of people (including a group of boys, one of whom I recognise as Matt) standing nearby, who had overheard what was said . . .

MRS COGG

At last it is time to go home. Mum has finished offending teachers – she even told Mrs Cogg, the IT teacher, that she had heard (from ME!!!) that her lessons were 'mind-numbingly boring' and advised her to seek an alternative career, possibly as a tea lady instead of an IT lady! Mum's 'little joke' went down like a lead balloon . . .

How can I EVER face anyone at school again? There is only one thing for it – I shall have to change schools (a school in Outer Mongolia would do – or one on the Planet Squarg, several trillion light years away from Little Bunbury . . .).

Worse still, how can I face Rio's parents? They must hate me now! I don't see how they can possibly still like me after what Mum said to them.

I am so hurt, angry and embarrassed that I don't say a word as we kangaroo-hop home in the Mini. But when we get home, I blurt out suddenly: 'Mum – how *could* you say all those things? Don't you understand what you've done? You've RUINED my life!!! Rio's parents are so . . . so . . . so nice!' I burst into tears. It is all too much to bear.

Mum looks surprised. 'I was only telling the truth, dear!'

'Then the truth STINKS!!! What did Mr Battlefield say? "Sometimes the truth is better left UNstated." It wasn't even the truth, most of the time. You went WAY over the top with all that stuff you said to Rio's parents! You don't even *know* them! Why are you acting so weird? It's really, really SCARY – and you don't seem to realise . . . *Please* – will you see a doctor? For *my* sake – before I go mad . . .' Tears stream down my face. I feel so helpless. And alone.

Mum comes over and puts her arms around me. 'I'll do anything for you, Maddy. So if you want me to see a doctor, I'll see a doctor – even though there's nothing wrong with me. There, there – dry your eyes! Just remember – I love you so very much.'

'I love you, too, Mum – and I want you back.'

'Want me back, dear? I haven't gone anywhere.'

(There is a strong smell of cat in the living room, and no sign of Augustus. Mum opens the window a little wider – she left it slightly open when we left and Augustus obviously pushed it open further and got out, jumping down on to the sloping roof over the entrance to the shop). Suddenly a weird, strangled cat noise drifts in through the window. It's probably Augustus singing male cat love songs into the night . . .

SINGING MALE CAT LOVE SONGS
INTO THE NIGHT . . .

'Mum – have you told Mrs Petheridge that we've got her cat?'

Mum avoids meeting my eye. (This is strange – recently she has been fixing people with a very direct gaze when voicing her strong opinions.)

'She came into the shop, dear,' says Mum. 'And she said that Augustus has taken to wandering off on his own, some-times for days at a time – and then he'll suddenly drop into her house for a meal, before disappearing again. He's obviously two-timing – cats do that. But she didn't seem too worried about him.'

'So you didn't tell her?'

'Um . . . I may have forgotten to mention it.'

So. Mum is capable of refraining from *complete* honesty when it suits her. (My heart does a strange sort of leap – could this be a small sign that Mum could return to normal? If only she could become aware of how weird her behaviour is, perhaps she could do something about it . . . I MUST keep trying to get through to her, no matter how hard it is . . .)

As I lie in bed, trying unsuccessfully to go to sleep, I suddenly see my life as a weird misshapen balloon, blown up out of proportion. There is a face on the balloon . . . a cross, frowning face . . . Mum's face! I have a pin (a LARGE pin) . . . BANG!!! The balloon disappears, and there is Mum, back to her normal shape and size, smiling at me . . . (I think this is called wishful thinking – or just weird thinking! But it helps – a little. Perhaps Mum WILL just snap back to normal one day . . .)

Chapter Nine

My Life Is Total Pants
(Big Green Ones . . .)

I WONDER how many people *won't* be talking to me today, after yesterday's disastrous parents' evening. I am worried about how Rio will have reacted, not to mention Mrs Cogg! (I am so worried that I try to get out of having to go to school or face anyone by saying that I have contracted a rare tropical disease from a delivery of bananas to the shop, and I don't want anyone to catch it. Mum tells me to stop talking nonsense and to go to school – she won't accept that I am suffering from Post-Traumatic Stress!)

Rio is subdued, but she is still talking to me!

'You don't need to worry, Maddy. Like I said, I know it's not *your* fault – and I was thinking how *I'd* feel if I had a mother like . . .'

'Like mine?'

'Oh! No! I didn't mean . . . sorry!' (For the first time that I can remember, Rio is stumbling over her words . . .)

'It's OK – I know what you mean. It's awful. Yesterday was awful. Today is going to be awful. Even the cat hates me! I expect your parents hate me – and Mum.'

'They don't hate *you*, Maddy! No one hates you! You mustn't think like that. You're such a lovely person. No one could possibly hate you . . .'

It's lunchbreak, and I'm being a loner. (I could probably go and talk to people if I made the effort, but I feel too upset – what if they're all talking behind my back?)

Oh, no – there's Hannah! And she's whispering to Rachel and Daisy, and they're looking at me . . . I want to run away . . . Hannah's coming over! I bet the other two have dared her to talk to me (like I'm really scary – with a mega-scary mother!).

I try to look bored, as if I couldn't care less about their silly, childish games.

'Er . . . Maddy?' says Hannah.

'Yes? What?' (I wish I had some fake fangs so that I could bare them at her and see her run away, screaming!)

'If you ever need someone to talk to, remember me – I'm still your friend, aren't I?' says Hannah tentatively. 'I . . . I thought you looked upset. By the way, I thought what your mum said to Mr Poole was really funny! Have you seen him today? He's shaved his beard off!'

I stop looking bored and look surprised. Hannah is being friendly!

'Rachel and Daisy are there, too. They still want to be friends with you. But we thought you didn't want to be friends with *us*. We thought we weren't cool enough for you!'

I look over to where Rachel and Daisy are standing,

looking back at me. They smile and wave in a frankly uncool manner – but it doesn't matter. The important thing is that they still like me! I don't feel much like talking, but it's good to know that I have friends.

'Thanks, Hannah!' I smile at her.

'It's OK.'

I am surprised to find that most of the teachers are nice to me – even the ones whom Mum was rude to. Mr Wheatengreen sounds concerned when he asks: 'Is your mother OK, Maddy? She didn't seem quite her usual self.'

'No, she's not,' I reply. 'She might have to see a doctor about it.' Then I make an excuse about not wanting to be late for my next lesson, and rush off, as I don't want to get into a discussion with Mr Wheatengreen about *why* Mum might have to see a doctor . . .

As I am preparing to go home, someone taps me on the shoulder. It is Matt, and he is with a group of boys (I recognise them as the ones who were listening in on Mum's verbal assault on Rio's parents). They are all grinning at me.

'Is your mum always as full on as that?' asks Matt.

'No . . .'

'Is it easy to wind her up?'

'What's it to you?' (Matt may be good-looking, but there is something about his manner which makes me edgy . . .)

'Nothing,' he says. 'Just wondered. Syd says she works in the Village Stores in Little Bunbury.'

MATT AND HIS FRIENDS

'Yes – we live there. So?'

'So I don't suppose she's got many customers left!' And they all roar with laughter and wander away.

'Do you think it would be OK with your mum and dad if I came home with you for a while?' I ask Rio on the bus, as we rattle home along the leafy country lanes.

'Um . . .' she hesitates.

'What's the matter? I thought you said they were OK.'

'I didn't say they were *OK* – I said that they didn't *hate* you. Mum and Dad don't hate people. They'd have to throw away their pipe of peace if they started doing that.'

'So, what's the problem?'

'They've . . . they've gone a bit funny!'

'Funny?'

'I don't mean like they've dressed up as clowns and they're throwing custard pies at each other – not that sort of funny . . .'

'So what, then?'

'They're all tight-lipped and not saying very much. They look stressed.'

'That's unfortunate – considering they run a de-stressing place. It's not a very good advert for it . . .'

'Exactly. But, joking apart, they don't really want us hanging out . . .'

'Oh, NO!!!' (I *need* Rio – and I want to see Syd, and I like Rio's mum and dad, and I thought they liked me . . .)

'I'm sorry, Maddy – but what can I do? They're my parents. Your mum seriously upset them, and they want me to keep my distance . . .'

'It's not FAIR! Why is EVERYONE against us? Can't you *talk* to your parents? I thought you were my friend . . .'

'Maddy! That's not fair! I AM your friend! Please . . .'

(But I have gone into Serious Sulk Mode . . .)

Walking home on my own after getting off the bus, I already feel stupid for overreacting – but it is all getting so difficult and complicated it's more than I can handle! (I am trying not to start crying again . . .)

I see Mrs Ploughman approaching, pushing her shopping trolley along. She must have just been to the Village Stores. (She does her shopping early on Saturday mornings, but she drops in every afternoon as well for a gossip and a

... SHE DOESN'T EVEN LOOK AT ME.

packet of McTwitties chocolate biscuits.) I hope that Mum hasn't offended her as well!

Is she going to say hello and remark on how much I've grown, like she always does?

No . . . Mrs Ploughman can't have failed to see me (she passes right by me), but she doesn't say a word – she doesn't even *look* at me. I feel like leaping out in front of her and shouting: 'Hello, Mrs Ploughman! It's ME – Maddy!! Look – I've GROWN!!!'

Mum has obviously said something to her. I can't stand it. I just want everything to go back to the way it was. I want people to go back to behaving the way they used to. It may have been boring – and sometimes irritating – but it was NORMAL.

* * *

'Mum – what did you say to Mrs Ploughman?'

'I told her that she was a gossipy old witch. That got rid of her!'

'Er, Mum? You're not supposed to get *rid* of the customers. This is a shop. We WANT customers. We're not going to have any money soon. Or any friends!'

Mum looks puzzled. 'Never mind, dear!' she says brightly. 'I've done something that should cheer you up!'

'Oh? What's that?'

'I've made an appointment.'

'Oh, Mum! That's BRILLIANT!' I rush over and give her a hug.

Mum laughs and hugs me back. 'I knew you'd be pleased!'

'When is it?'

'Tomorrow! He's having his goolies chopped off first thing tomorrow.'

'Er . . . what?'

'Augustus. I'm taking your advice and having him neutered. Then the room won't smell. I've cleared it with Mrs Petheridge, by the way – I told her that her cat had moved in with us. She didn't seem to mind at all – in fact she seemed almost relieved. But then she said something about buying her cat food elsewhere in future.'

122

'MUM!!! I . . . I thought you meant that you'd made an appointment for *you*.'

'Oh, no, dear. Not yet. Plenty of time for that, especially since there's nothing wrong with me! I thought it was more important to get Augustus sorted out, don't you . . .?'

(No.)

'Mum!!! Oh – I give up . . .'

Since I'm no longer welcome at Rio's house (I feel a great stab of hurt every time I think of this), and Uncle Nigel is about the only 'normal' person left in my life, I decide to go and visit him and Aunty Ann. Aunty Ann is still in a huff (it is a very long huff – a World Record huff) and sits with her arms folded, watching *Weekenders* and ignoring me. (*Weekenders* is on every weekday but not at weekends – make any sense?!)

Uncle Nigel makes a great fuss of me, welcoming me in and making me cocoa and offering me all sorts of biscuits and cakes, and asking how I am, and how I'm getting on at school (he doesn't *just* talk about Mum – which is a relief!). He is so nice – he's like Mum *used* to be (you can tell that they're brother and sister). He lets me send an e-mail to Rio. (She gave me her e-mail address, just in case Mum and I joined the Real World and got a computer . . .) I tell her that I'm sorry for going off in a stress, but the whole situation is getting to me . . . she e-mails back to say that the situation is getting to *her*, too, but that we should both try to stay cool and be friends . . .

It is getting late, and I don't really want to go home, but Uncle Nigel says that I must.

'You're the most "normal" part of Helen's life at the moment, Maddy,' he says, 'and it's very important that you go on being there for her – she's depending on you . . .'

This is an odd thought (almost as odd as my 'balloon' thought!). I am still trying to get my head around it as I lie in bed, waiting for sleep to overwhelm my poor, tired brain . . .

Chapter Ten

Rio to the Rescue!
(And Syd! And Jack!)

MUM IS angry because Uncle Nigel let slip that I used his computer to send e-mails. It took ages to convince Mum that I had *not* engaged in correspondence with some perv or other whom I had met over the Internet. (That would be *so* disgusting! It would be a blee!-mail . . .) She wasn't *much* happier when I finally managed to convince her that the only person whom I had been e-mailing was Rio. Now she seems to be sulking and ignoring me, concentrating instead on Augustus, who is recovering from his operation this morning. It feels weird – as if Mum is the moody teenager and I am the adult. It's not RIGHT – I want it to be the other way round!!!

Friday

In a bid to placate Mum, I go to choir practice this evening as usual – but I feel as if all the other members of the choir are staring at me. (I suppose I *could* be imagining it . . .)

Uncle Nigel comes round later in the evening (Aunty Ann is refusing to come anywhere near Mum – or Augustus) and I overhear him in the kitchen, trying to persuade Mum to go to the doctor – but without success. (Mum is still cross with Uncle Nigel for allowing me to use his computer to send e-mails without her permission.)

Saturday

I do my paper round this morning, and NO ONE says hello to me – not a single person. (True – it is raining, and there aren't many people about. But Mr Battlefield walks straight past and

PING!
AN IDEA OCCURS!

doesn't raise his hat *or* his umbrella to me!) And, to rub salt into the wound, Rio's mum and dad drive past in their car and they don't even look at me.

Then, suddenly – PING! An idea occurs to me – Rio's parents are OUT. I could go and see Rio! (And Syd . . .)

It's a bit risky, but I needn't stay for too long – hopefully Rio's parents and my mum will never know. And I want to spend some time on my own with Rio (not on the bus and without Kate and Jaz waffling on about their boyfriends all through lunchbreak). I just need a friend – a good friend, like Rio. (And I might even get to see Syd in his dressing gown!!!)

Syd opens the door of Marsh Cottage – he is fully dressed (shame), and his hair looks more tousled than usual (sexee!!!).

'Hi, Maddy! Are you going to stand there all day or are you coming in?'

'I . . . I'm not supposed to be here . . .'

'Oh, don't worry about Mum and Dad! They've got some serious chilling to do! Come in! Jack's here – he stayed with us last night – we stayed up playing on the Playstation all night. That's why we're already up and dressed – we didn't go to bed at all!'

Jack is sitting at the kitchen table, sorting through a pile of CDs.

'Hello, Maddy!'

'Hello, Jack!'

Syd looks thoughtful. 'I've just had an idea!' he says.

'That must be a first,' comments Jack.

'Shut up!' says Syd good-humouredly. 'I just thought – since Maddy's worried about Mum and Dad finding her here, why don't we wake up my lazy lump of a little sister, and we could all go out on a picnic? It's stopped raining now, and the sun's shining – I think it's going to be hot.'

'Great idea!' enthuses Jack.

'Cool!' I say. (A picnic with SYD!!! And Jack! Yes!!! It's about time something NICE happened to me . . .)

Rio is surprised, but seems pleased, when I knock on her door and go in. I tell her that I'm sorry for being such a grumpy-guts, and it's probably time I lightened up. She tells me not to worry – she understands what I'm going through. She says that she realises that my mum probably can't help it – it was because of the accident, and maybe she'll be better soon – and Rio also says that she'll try to explain all this to her parents. Then we agree that parents can be a pain, even at the best of times – and turn our minds to happier thoughts . . .

'A picnic? With Jack?!! YUM!!!' says Rio with relish . . .

Soon we are walking up the hill towards Little Bunbury. Syd tells us that there is a turning off the road, just before we get

128

to the village itself, which leads into a patch of woodland and then open fields and views across Bunbury Vale. The boys are carrying backpacks full of provisions.

We find a patch of stony ground (the grass is still damp) and Syd unrolls the groundsheet that he was carrying with his backpack. Rio and I sit on it, and Jack sits down too. Rio is doing some *very* obvious, *uncool* ogling. Syd picks up a backpack and empties the contents over our heads.

'Hey!' we shout, as packets of McTwitties chocolate biscuits and bags of crisps rain down on us. There is also a large chunk of Insanely Strong Cheddar and a jar of pickle (which narrowly misses hitting me on the head!).

'What do you think you're doing, Syd?' Rio shouts at her

brother. 'You nearly hit Maddy on the head with a jar of pickle! That could have been even worse than a cricket ball – sorry, Maddy!'

'Sorry!' says Syd, sitting down next to me. (I feel FINE!!!)

'Where are the sandwiches?' Rio asks.

'Sandwiches?' exclaims Syd. 'You seriously expect me to have made *sandwiches*?'

'No, I suppose not,' says Rio. 'But what are we supposed to eat, apart from biscuits and crisps? I thought this was going to be a *proper* picnic. But there's just . . . cheese.'

'And pickle!'

'What have you got in your backpack, Jack?' I ask.

'More cheese. And some bananas. And extra crisps, in case we run out.'

'For goodness' sake!' says Rio.

'Look – you eat it like this!' says Syd. He breaks off a large piece of cheddar cheese and dips it straight into the pickle jar, scooping out an enormous dollop of pickle and putting the whole lot in his mouth in one go. 'Mmmmm!!!'

Rio stares at her brother in disgust. (I gaze at him adoringly – I really go for a man who can handle his cheese!)

Syd seems to be breaking out in a slight sweat . . .

'I hardly like to mention this,' says Rio, 'but did anyone bring anything to drink?'

'Ah.'

'Er . . .'

'I'll take that as a no, then, shall I?'

'OK, OK!' says Syd. 'Drop the sarcasm, Rio! All you've

done is moan and complain, ever since we got here. It's not as if you even helped with the preparations or anything!'

(It must be nice to have a brother or sister – someone to argue with! I can't help wishing that I had a brother or sister so that I wouldn't be all on my own with Mum, especially as she is at the moment . . .)

'We could go and buy some Coke or something. I've got a few pounds,' says Jack.

'You don't mean . . . ?' Syd begins.

'From the Village Stores?' Rio finishes the question that was on all our minds. (Jack might just as well have suggested going to get drinks from the Castle of Doom over the Lonely Mountains and into the Valley of Dread – he would have got the same reaction.) Now they are all looking at *me*.

'No,' I say flatly. 'I am *not* going to the Village Stores for drinks. If Mum even suspects that I'm with you lot, she'll never let me out again!'

'Well, I'm not going on my *own*,' says Jack.

'Oh, for goodness' sake! I can't believe what a bunch of wimps you're all being!' exclaims Syd scornfully. '*I'll* go – I mean, how scary can Maddy's mum be?!'

There is an awkward silence.

'I know,' says Syd. 'You lot can hide behind the cricket pavilion, and you can come and rescue me if she starts breathing fire over me.'

'Syd! Honestly!' Rio rebukes her brother. 'Sorry, Maddy!'

'It's OK.' (I know that Syd is only teasing – in a friendly way, unlike Matt. But I am trying not to show my friends how hurt and embarrassed I feel at having the sort of mum whom no one wants to go near . . . Life was so much easier before . . . I try to make light of it . . .) 'She doesn't bite,' I say. 'Just don't ask her how she is . . .'

We decide to do what Syd suggested, so we pack up the picnic and head for the village green. Soon we are lurking behind the cricket pavilion, while Syd wanders over to the shop.

'Hey! Isn't that Matt over there?' says Rio. 'He's going into the shop with those friends of his – Wayne and Dan. I want to see them – I'm going over . . .'

'Rio!' I call after her – but she is running towards the shop. (Isn't it uncool to chase boys . . . ?)

'Oh, well – might as well go and join them,' says Jack, and he sets off across the green.

(AAAAARGH!!! What is the *matter* with my friends? Mum is bound to have a go at them . . . But I don't want to hang around behind the cricket pavilion on my own . . .)

With a feeling of foreboding, I wander slowly towards the Village Stores. I can hear shouting and laughing coming from inside the shop – the laughter sounds over-loud and unfriendly. I hear Rio shout 'Shut up!' (What on earth has Mum been saying *this* time?!)

A kind of horrified fascination impels me to open the door and step inside.

Mum is behind the counter, and Matt, Wayne and Dan are standing just in front of it with stupid grins on their faces.

'WHAT did you just call Dan, Mrs Mitchell?' asks Matt, choking with laughter.

'I called him an IDIOTIC, BRAIN-DEAD WASTE OF SPACE WITH THE CHARM AND LOOKS OF A BABOON!' shouts Mum (she looks flustered, even . . . frightened). 'And YOU . . .' she adds to Matt, '*you* are a very rude and unpleasant boy who *thinks* he's clever – but you're a MORON! You have all the social graces of a SKUNK!'

Matt, Wayne and Dan hoot with laughter. 'Oh, that was *very* polite!' says Matt mockingly. 'I'm sure you can do better than *that*! Come on – what was that VERY rude word you said just now? *Please* remind me . . .'

I quickly realise that it was not *Mum* whom Rio was telling to shut up – it was Matt and his friends. Rio looks furious. 'They're treating your mum like she's some kind of freak show!' she hisses at me. '*Do* something, Syd!'

'Come on, Jack!' Syd mutters, and both boys walk over to Matt, Wayne and Dan and tap them on the shoulders.

'Out!' Syd says to them, jerking his head towards the door.

'Hey, Syd!' exclaims Matt, trying to be all matey – as if nothing has been going on. 'We were just having a laugh with Maddy's mum – you're a good sport, Mrs M!'

'You weren't laughing *with* her, you were laughing *at* her!' shouts Rio angrily. 'You're a bunch of freaks!' (Rio is expressing how I feel. Mum looks so vulnerable, and I feel a sudden urge to protect her and look after her – and a slight twinge of guilt that all I seem to have been concerned about up until now is myself, and that Mum should look after *me*!)

'Wow! Your kid sister's a bit mouthy, isn't she?' says Matt. 'Just like Maddy. What was it you called me, Maddy? FAT

ARSE! That was it! And now I know where you get it from!' He grins nastily at Mum.

'GET OUT!' shouts Jack. He has stepped forward so that he is face to face with Matt. There is something about the expression on his face, combined with the lip-ring and eyebrow piercing, which makes him look like Someone Who Should Not Be Argued With . . .

'OK, OK!' exclaims Matt, raising his hands in a submissive gesture. 'We were just leaving! Some people just don't know how to take a joke!' he adds, over his shoulder, as he and his friends leave the shop.

Rio rushes over to the door and yells after them: 'And don't come back!'

JACK IS A HERO!

(I feel like a wimp. I just stood there and said nothing while all of this was going on – but I was too shocked. Now I walk over to Mum and touch her gently on the arm . . .)

'Are you OK, Mum?' She looks pale and tired.

'Yes, Maddy. I'll be fine. And thank you . . .'

She looks at me, and then at Jack, Syd and Rio. 'Thank you!' she says again. 'You got rid of those unpleasant boys. I think . . .' Mum pauses (she seems to be struggling to say something that is difficult for her). 'I think I owe you an apology.' (She is mainly addressing Jack). 'I may have misjudged you. I still don't like your lip-ring, or the one in your eyebrow, but you were kind to me just now. Thank you.'

'It's OK!' says Jack, 'Really . . .'

Mum turns to look at Syd and Rio. 'You both stood up for me as well,' she says. 'And you must be nice young people, to be friends with him . . .' (She nods at Jack, who seems to have become Mum's hero!) 'I shouldn't have said what I said to your parents – I will apologise to them when I see them.' Now Mum turns to me. 'Maddy . . .'

'Yes, Mum?'

'You've been right all along, dear,' she says, putting her arm around me. 'I think I *should* go to the doctor's – I seem to have, er, developed a tendency to . . . to overreact. I really *don't* like upsetting people, you know.' She shakes her head sadly. 'I'm sorry for misjudging your friends – they seem to be OK. But don't copy their hair, the way they dress, or plaster make-up all over your face, or drill holes in your lip, nose or eyebrows.'

Out of the corner of my eye I can see that Rio's mouth is twitching, and I am aware that my friends are trying not to laugh . . . but it is not unfriendly laughter, although it may be nervous! At least Mum is making an effort to be nice. I hardly dare to hope – but could she be showing the first signs of returning to normal? That would be sooooooo amazing . . .

Mum goes on being nice. She refuses to accept payment for a two-litre bottle of Coke and the bars of chocolate which we put on the counter. She also fetches a comb from a stand near the counter, and pushes it towards Syd. 'So that you can comb your hair,' she says.

'Er . . . thanks!' (Syd takes the comb, blushing slightly – the fact that he blushes makes me love him even more!)

Mum seems reluctant for us to leave. 'It's been so quiet here!' she says with a sigh. 'I don't seem to have any customers. Mrs MacGregor-Willey came in earlier, but she left without buying anything after I asked her how she came to have such a ridiculous name.'

Mum sighs and looks sadly down at the counter. 'I didn't want to worry you, Maddy, but business hasn't been good. I'm not sure how we're going to keep going.'

The expression on my face must be registering Extreme Worry – does Mum mean we're going to lose our home? I feel sick.

Rio glances at me, and then she looks thoughtful. 'Come on, Maddy! Come on, Syd, Jack . . .'

* * *

We're all racing down the hill towards Marsh Cottage, following Rio.

'This had better be good!' shouts Syd. 'I'm carrying a whole picnic, including a full bottle of Coke, in my backpack, and I hadn't planned to go for a run!'

We come to a halt, puffing and panting, outside the front door of Marsh Cottage.

'The only way . . .' gasps Rio, '. . . to deal with this situation is to be HONEST!'

'Honest?' I query.

'Yes! Honest! Meet it head on and DEAL WITH IT!'

'Right . . . How?' I ask.

'TELL people! *Explain!*'

'But it's . . . sort of embarrassing . . .'

'Well – what's worse? Being embarrassed, or letting things get so bad that your mum loses her business? You and your mum need people to *understand* – then they'll stop getting offended all the time, and they'll start going back to the shop. Right?'

'Right,' I say slowly. (But I can't help thinking that it's still not going to be comfortable for people, hearing what Mum really thinks . . .)

But Jack looks convinced. 'Rio's right,' he says.

(Rio visibly melts, and a dreamy look comes into her eyes – Jack just AGREED with her! Then she recovers . . .)

'Come on!' she says. 'Let's start with Mum and Dad! Their car's here, so they must be back from shopping.'

* * *

Rio confronts her parents in the kitchen. 'I want a family pow-wow!' she says. 'Right now! And Maddy and Jack must be allowed to join in. It's about Maddy . . . and her mum.'

Rio's parents look taken aback. 'Well – if it's important to you, dear,' says her dad.

'It is.'

'I'll go and fetch the pipe of peace,' says her mum . . .

It doesn't take very much passing of the pipe of peace before Rio's parents reassure me about the whole situation. They tell me that they had already worked out that there must be something wrong with Mum – but that they hadn't wanted to interfere in case they made matters worse, since Mum didn't seem to like them very much. Rio's dad also apologises for letting their own offended feelings get in the way, but if I would like their help they will see what they can do . . .

Chapter Eleven

Back to 'Normal'

MUM IS driving me mad. She keeps going on and on about Jack and how wonderful he is, and how she wouldn't mind if I went out with him because she is certain that he is a responsible boy who would look after me, and get me home at a sensible time. 'And you could probably persuade him to get rid of that dreadful lipring, and the equally unsightly one on his eyebrow,' she says enthusiastically. 'He'd be quite good-looking without *those*! Did you say he does beatboxing? He must be very fit.' (Mum obviously thinks that beatboxing is some kind of martial art.)

'Yes, Mum – Jack is very fit. So's Syd.' (But not in the sense Mum means! Syd is FIT!)

Mum and I are at cross purposes – but at least it's a friendly conversation. I try to get through to Mum that Jack is not interested in me (in that way) and I am not interested in *him* (in that way . . . If I *was* interested in him, I think Mum would have put me off by now! She likes him *too* much!).

Changing the subject, Mum tells me that she is going to the doctor's first thing tomorrow. (YES!)

* * *

I don't want to go to church, but Mum insists that we both go. My heart sinks at the thought of all the unfriendly looks that we are going to get, from the other choir members and from the people in the congregation who used to be Mum's regular customers (the entire congregation, that is). Mum even managed to offend the vicar – Reverend Witherspoon – when he came into the shop before choir practice on Friday to buy sugar, biscuits, orange squash, a large bag of mint humbugs and another of assorted toffees, as treats and refreshments for

the choir members. She told him off for buying so many high-sugar foods and said that God would punish him for caring so little for the teeth of his parishioners.

But Rio's parents (who – unusually – are at church today with Syd and Rio) have obviously had a word with Reverend Witherspoon, and (it would seem) with one or two members of the congregation. As I crouch down low and try to sink into the choir stalls without Syd seeing me, I notice people smiling at Mum in a friendly way! After the service, they crowd around her, asking her how she is, wishing her well and assuring her that they will be in the Village Stores doing their shopping first thing tomorrow. Mum looks flustered at all the attention – but pleased. Uncle Nigel and Aunty Ann are among the well-wishers. Aunty Ann looks slightly unwilling, as if Uncle Nigel has talked her into it . . .

From a distance (they are just leaving the church), I see Rio and her parents smiling at me. I smile back, and mouth the words 'thank you' at them. Syd must already have left – I don't think Syd and church go together very naturally – but suddenly he puts his head round the church door and gives me a cheery grin and waves. I feel myself blushing the same colour as my . . . CASSOCK!!! With a little squeak, I rush away to the vestry to take the stupid garment *off*! Why can't I ever look cool when Syd's around?! (Still – I know that I'm lucky to have such good friends, Syd included . . .)

As I leave the church, Mrs Ploughman, who has been talking to Mum, exclaims: 'Maddy! Goodness me – I can't believe how much you've grown!' And Mr Battlefield passes by, raising his hat. Life is certainly returning to normal – but is Mum returning to normal, too? She seems to have managed to get through the morning without being rude to anyone. She has even apologised to nearly everyone (apart from Aunty Ann), and told Uncle Nigel about the doctor's appointment tomorrow.

'She seems a lot more like her usual self, don't you think?' Uncle Nigel whispers to me. I nod, although I am not completely reassured . . .

'Oh, look!' says Mum loudly, as Aunty Ann wobbles away through the church gates (she obviously didn't want to stay and chat). 'There goes Mrs Blobby!'

Uncle Nigel sighs heavily and shakes his head. 'Honestly, Helen!' he says. I don't think that Mum is *quite* back to normal . . .

Mum keeps her doctor's appointment on Monday morning. When I get home from school, she tells me that the doctor has told her that, in his opinion, the effects of her injury will wear off gradually, along with the persistent headaches, and he has prescribed painkillers.

'The headaches *aren't* as bad as they were,' says Mum, smiling. 'I feel *so* much better now that I've taken your advice, Maddy, and Uncle Nigel's, and seen the doctor. I may even have counselling – that was something else the doctor suggested. I'm so sorry to have put you – and the customers! – through all of this!'

'That's OK, Mum – it's not your fault . . .'

I am so glad that Mum has faced up to what has been going on and is being honest with herself. Suddenly I realise that this has been her thing all along – honesty. This can be good *and* bad, depending on where and when and to whom she voices her honest opinions!

At lunchbreak on Tuesday, Matt swaggers up to me, followed closely by a grinning Wayne and Dan.

'How's your mum, Maddy?' Matt asks tauntingly. 'Has she said any more *rude* words?' He smirks, aware that people around us are listening.

'Get lost, MORON!' I say loudly.

'Ooooooh!' he exclaims, drawing in his breath in mock offence. 'Like mother, like daughter!'

I turn my back on him and walk away without another word. I feel shaky but pleased that I put him in his place (slightly lower than a particularly slimy, icky earthworm! An earthworm with bleached hair.).

Hannah, Rachel and Daisy run after me and gaze at me in awe.

'Wow, Maddy!' exclaims Rachel. 'That was *so* cool!'

'I *know*! Isn't it great?' We all start giggling in a slightly less cool manner. (I have decided

AN EARTHWORM WITH BLEACHED HAIR ...

that the coolest thing to do is to hang out with the Cool Crowd *and* with the Slightly Less Cool Crowd – they are all my friends, or, at least, most of them are.)

I ask Rio if she'd like to come back to my place after school, and she says yes. Mum has said that she doesn't mind any more, as long as Rio and I promise not to sing! I have also agreed to keep the music turned down, in order to avoid giving any of the elderly customers a heart attack . . . Mum has relaxed enough to allow Rio and me to hang out together and do stuff, like going for a milkshake in the nearest big town, Leatherbridge.

A strange and unexpected sight greets us as we walk into the living room. Mum is sitting on the sofa with her arm around . . .

MUM HAS RELAXED ENOUGH TO
ALLOW RIO AND ME TO HANG
OUT TOGETHER AND DO STUFF,
LIKE GOING FOR A MILK-SHAKE
IN THE NEAREST BIG TOWN, LEATHERBRIDGE

Aunty Ann! Aunty Ann is wobbling convulsively, sobbing into
a handful of tissues from the box that Mum is offering her. I
start panicking – what if something has happened to Uncle
Nigel? I couldn't bear it!

'Mum! Wh . . . what's happened?'

'It's Foofy, dear.'

Aunty Ann erupts into anguished sobs.

'There, there, dear!' says Mum soothingly, giving her a hug.
'Foofy's in heaven now. He wouldn't like to see you so upset.'

Aunty Ann nods and blows her nose, trumpet-like, into a
fresh hanky clutched in her plump hand.

Noticing the shocked expression on my face (Foofy has been part of my life for so long – now he's gone . . .), Mum explains. 'He had a heart attack, darling. It was very sudden – he didn't suffer. I met Nigel and Ann at the vet's when I went to get some flea treatment for Gus . . .'

THERE THERE!

A STRANGE AND UNEXPECTED SIGHT – MUM IS COMFORTING AUNTY ANN !

'We took Foofy straight . . . straight to the vet,' sobs Aunty Ann. 'But it was . . . too . . . late!' She dissolves into more floods of tears, leaning her head against Mum's shoulder. Mum looks . . . squashed.

Rio puts her arm around me. 'Are you OK, Maddy?' she asks. I nod. I *am* sad about Foofy, and feel sorry for Aunty Ann – but

I can't help feeling a sense of overwhelming relief at the sight of Mum behaving like her old nice, kind self – oh, if only it lasts!!! That would be so great!)

Augustus is curled up in an armchair, sleeping peacefully.

Mum looks thoughtful. 'I've got an idea, Ann!' she says.

'What?' asks Aunty Ann, sniffing.

'Well – you and Nigel were kind enough to let Maddy and I share Foofy with you for all those years . . . Why don't you share Augustus with us? He can be *your* cat, too.'

Aunty Ann gazes at Augustus blearily. 'He can never take the place of Foofy,' she says.

'Oh, no!' exclaims Mum. 'I wasn't suggesting he *should* . . .'

'But . . . but it's kind of you, Helen,' Aunty Ann continues. 'And I suppose he *is* rather sweet . . .'

(SWEET?!! There are a number of words I can think of to describe Augustus – not all of them polite – but 'sweet' is not one of them.)

'Yes, he's really cute, isn't he?' agrees Rio. (I realise that she hasn't met Augustus before.) Walking across the room, she perches on the edge of the armchair so that she can stroke his fluffy head. 'Who's a lovely boy?' she coos. 'Who's a gorgeous porgeous furry fellow?! What HANDSOME whiskers you've got!'

(Oh, well. I hadn't thought Rio was the sort of girl who'd go all gooey over an enormous ginger cat with a torn ear and a scar over his eye – but you can never tell! I suppose if cats went in for body-piercing, Augustus is the sort of cat who'd have his ears, eyebrows, nose *and* lip pierced . . .)

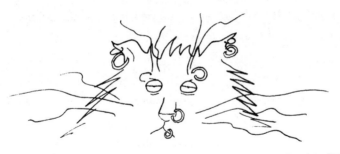

AUGUSTUS IS THE SORT OF CAT WHO'D
HAVE HIS EARS, EYEBROWS, NOSE <u>AND</u>
LIP PIERCED . . .

Gently manoeuvring herself away from Aunty Ann, Mum joins Rio in making a big fuss of Augustus. Aunty Ann falls forward on to the sofa, face down in a cushion, and continues to sob.

I go out to the kitchen to make tea for Mum and Aunty Ann – I feel like doing something 'normal' and everydayish, just to celebrate!

I wonder what brought about the return of Mum's usual self? Perhaps it was the shock of Foofy's death, and seeing Aunty Ann so distressed – or perhaps it is just another example of Mum's tendency to extreme honesty. Her innermost feeling today is obviously compassion for Aunty Ann, and she is expressing it quite openly (leaving me with a small, nagging doubt that a few days – or moments – from now she could just as easily express her earlier opinion that Aunty Ann looks like Mrs Blobby . . .)

As I hand Mum her cup of tea, she smiles at me. 'Thank you, Maddy, darling! Thank you for the tea, and . . . and for everything!' She gets up and gives me a big hug. 'Remember – I love you!' she whispers in my ear.

'I love you, too, Mum!'

It is a hot, sunny Friday afternoon, and Rio and I have just got off the school bus. Rio wants a two-litre bottle of Coke to take home with her, so we wander into Mum's shop, which is full of customers.

A customer called Mrs Fforbes-Ffortescue walks into the shop, wearing a wide-brimmed straw hat decorated with flowers, fruit and ostrich feathers (she has to tilt her head slightly in order to get through the doorway with her hat still on).

'What a ridiculous hat!' exclaims Mum loudly. Then she catches my eye . . . 'Er . . . hat . . . hattitude!' she stammers. 'What a ridiculous hattitude . . . I mean attitude the council has taken over the proposal to build a public convenience on the village green!'

'I didn't know there *was* a proposal to build a public convenience on the village green,' says Mrs Fforbes-Ffortescue.

'Exactly!' exclaims Mum, warming to her theme. 'We haven't been consulted – the Council is keeping us in the dark!'

'You mean there aren't going to be any lights in the public convenience?' asks Mrs Partridge, looking confused.

'Scandalous!' roars Mr Battlefield, making us all jump. 'I shall write to the council immediately! Good day to you!' And he shuffles out, raising his hat.

I feel in need of some fresh air before I have to go to choir practice, so I walk with Rio back to her house.

'So your mum's still saying weird stuff?' says Rio.

'Yes – but she's not as bad as she was. Most of the time she's pretty normal. Except that I'm not sure what "normal" *is* any more! She *still* won't let me have my belly-button pierced – I've told her that *everyone* has their belly-buttons pierced these days, except me. But she's still saying no. That's pretty normal for Mum, I suppose . . .'

We reach Marsh Cottage, and I follow Rio into the kitchen to put the Coke in the fridge. Syd is there! He is sitting at the kitchen table, eating a sandwich, and raises his hand – and his sandwich – in greeting.

'Maddy!'

'H . . . hello, Syd!' (I try to sound casual – I don't want Syd to know that I fancy him like mad and I don't want Rio to tease me endlessly for fancying her brother . . .)

'By the way, Maddy,' says Syd, 'I've been meaning to say something to you, ever since the spring concert . . .'

(Uh-oh – what? I *know* I looked like a total IDIOT . . .)

Syd smiles at me. 'Don't look so worried!' he says. 'You've got a fabulous voice. Can I be your agent when you're rich and famous? But seriously – you sing really well!'

I feel myself blushing. I try to say thank you but unfortunately my voice goes very strange and the 'thank' comes out as a squeak, while the 'you' comes out as a croak (combined Mouse and Frog Syndrome. I don't understand why it is that I can get up and sing in front of people and then make such a mess of saying something simple like 'thank you').

'Did you see the video I made of the concert?' Syd asks. 'I gave it to Rio to give to Mr Crotchett.'

'Yes, we watched it during one of our lessons,' I reply. 'It was very good.'

Rio snorts derisively. 'Apart from the fact that you chopped all our heads off!' she says. 'And the stage seemed to be on a slant – I'm surprised we didn't slide off the end.'

'OK, OK!' exclaims Syd. 'It was meant to be artistic, with interesting camera angles – OK? I'd like to see *you* make a better video, Rio!'

(I am cringing slightly at the memory of seeing myself singing the 'fishy' song – *why* did Syd have to film THAT?! And in the song I did with Rio I just look MAD. No other word for it . . .)

'I've been thinking,' Syd begins. 'NO rude comments, please! I do a lot of thinking – people don't realise. But I thought we ought to have another go at having a picnic, especially since our last one got cut short . . . We'll do it properly this time. I *can* make sandwiches! I know – we'll have baguettes . . .'

'With cheese and pickle?'

'Great idea, Rio!' Syd gives her a thumbs up sign. 'I texted Jack, and asked him if he'd like to come, and he texted back to say yes – he could make it tomorrow. And the weather's supposed to be good this weekend – after that it's going to rain. So would you like to come, Maddy?'

(WOULD I?!!! I want to do handsprings around the kitchen,

shout 'RESULT!!! YESSSS!!!' and give Syd *the* most enormous hug – but I suppose that wouldn't be cool . . .)

'Yes, OK!' I say, as casually as I can. (Could this picnic be considered a *date*? WITH SYD?)

The following day . . . sitting on a rug under a cloudless blue sky . . . munching a cheese and pickle baguette . . . with Rio, Jack and Syd . . . Syd sitting close to me, but slightly turned away, so I can gaze at him to my heart's content without him realising (I can put up with Rio grinning and pulling faces at me!) . . . I feel happy to be with my friends . . . and I feel happy that Mum is getting better . . . and that Mr Battlefield is raising his hat to us again . . . and I feel happy to be ME . . .

And that's the honest truth!

If you would like more information about
books available from Piccadilly Press and
how to order them, please contact us at:

Piccadilly Press Ltd.
5 Castle Road
London
NW1 8PR

Tel: 020 7267 4492
Fax: 020 7267 4493

Feel free to visit our website at
www.piccadillypress.co.uk